Unexpected Mergers

THE ALEXANDER PROPOSAL

LORI FAYRE

The Alexander Proposal
ISBN # 978-1-83943-923-0
©Copyright Lori Fayre 2020
Cover Art by Louisa Maggio ©Copyright October 2020
Interior text design by Claire Siemaszkiewicz
Totally Bound Publishing

THE
ALEXANDER
PROPOSAL

Dedication

To every reader who has a guilty pleasure genre

Chapter One

July 1

Jade's phone rang, a shrill sound that cut through the silence of her office. She answered in a distracted tone, her eyes glued to her computer screen, "Yes?"

"Miss Saunders," her secretary's voice said, "your father needs you in his office. He wants to talk to you immediately."

That was strange. *Have I done something wrong?*

"Thank you, Carol. Please tell him I'll be right there." She set the phone back down on the cradle and tapped her pen against the desk in front of her. With a short breath, Jade stood and made her way down the hall to Timothy Saunders' office, letting herself in without knocking.

Jade's office was situated only a few doors down from her father's, but today it had seemed leagues away. While her space was small and to the point, void of any frills or decoration, Timothy had decked out his rich wood-paneled office with dark-leather furniture and cozy rugs. Jade drifted her gaze over the dozens of framed family pictures that covered his walls. Staring back at her was her own face, younger and chubbier with missing teeth. As she closed in on her father's desk, the pictures morphed, both herself and her parents aging until she reached the last one.

Jade stilled for a moment, taking in a photo from Miami a few summers before. There she was, between her parents with the beach behind them. Her long black hair was pulled back in a ponytail, her fair skin tinged pink from the Florida sun and her light green eyes bright. The three of them looked so happy in that picture. Now, Jade felt a surge of sadness when she looked at it. This time next year, both Timothy and Angela Saunders would be living in Miami permanently to enjoy a retired life, while she stayed in Dallas.

"Jade…" Timothy's soft voice pulled Jade from her thoughts. He was watching her, a question lingering in his stormy-gray eyes. "Is everything all right?" It was only then that she realized she had been standing there for several seconds, staring at the photograph.

"Sorry," she said. "Just got lost, I guess." Jade let out a nervous laugh and settled into one of the overstuffed leather chairs in the room, smoothing her charcoal pencil skirt over her legs. Her father probably knew what she had been thinking about, but he didn't mention it any further.

"We need to talk, Jade." Timothy used a tone that she recognized.

"What happened?" Jade's mind automatically went to her mother, who had always been prone to illness.

"It's nothing to worry about," he said, raising his palms in emphasis. "But I do want you to prepare yourself and…keep an open mind." Jade angled herself so that her father had her full attention. "Jade, you know that I've been in talks with Carlton Alexander, yes?"

"Of course. The Alexanders are looking to contract some business from us, right?"

Timothy grimaced, folding his hands in front of him.

"Not exactly." He took a deep breath, obviously preparing himself for whatever bombshell he was about to drop. "Carlton wants to buy Saunders Metalwork."

Jade blinked in surprise.

What in the world would Alexander International want with a Texas-based metal company?

"I mean, it's unusual, but it shouldn't be a problem, right?" Jade stood, pacing the room in her black heels. Was he telling her this because she was on the Board of Directors? Or because she was the CEO-elect? "Will it have much of an effect on your retirement plans?"

"No, it will actually help in that aspect." Timothy smiled, a flash of white teeth under his graying mustache. "But there is one catch. Do you remember their son Spencer?"

Jade huffed. It was hard to forget someone like him.

Spencer was two years her senior, but they had always been good friends — until Jade turned eighteen and had decided it was time to confess her feelings for him, until she had been rejected and hadn't spoken to the Alexanders for seven years as a result. She could still feel the burning humiliation of that day, and she crossed her arms as though that could protect her from the memories.

"Yes, I remember him." Her voice was clipped and cold, causing Timothy to sigh and lean back in his chair.

"Well, he will be taking over Alexander International in October." Now, *that* was a surprise. It seemed as though the Saunders and Alexanders were retiring around the same time. Jade couldn't help but wonder if they'd planned it all. Then the potential repercussions of what he'd said struck her.

"Please, tell me I'm not going to have to work for Spencer." She groaned. "Dad, you don't know what happened between us. It would be…awkward." She stood, lacing her fingers together nervously.

"You're a grown woman now, Jade, and I am proud of you. But you have got to learn to let go of the past, sweetheart." Timothy stood from his chair, circled the enormous desk and placed his hands on her shoulders. "Trust me when I tell you this is all for the best. Now, are you ready to hear the details of the proposal?" Jade closed her eyes. Even if she retained some executive rights, having Spencer as her boss would be bad enough. *How much worse can it get?*

"I'm ready," Jade finally said, opening her eyes to look at her father. He didn't waste any time sugar-coating his words.

"There is a clause in the contract that says you have to marry Spencer by the end of September." The words were rushed but clear. Still, it took Jade nearly a full minute for his statement to sink in. She bit back a laugh.

"Is that a joke? Because it's a bad one." Her father's eyes were glassy, as though the news upset him as much as it did her. Any trace of humor left her as she stared at him. "Dad, you can't expect… Do you know what year it is?"

"I know," he said. "It isn't unheard of, though. And Carlton and I have our reasons."

"Are you seriously agreeing with this?" Jade's voice pitched higher. She was being loud, but she couldn't care, not then.

Ignoring her question, Timothy continued.

"In four days, you'll be heading to New York, where you will oversee the deal, get the lie of the land and get to know Spencer better." The room began to tilt around Jade, and she reached out for something to steady herself. Timothy led her over to a couch and had her sit down. "I know it's a lot, but I promise you that it's all for the best." She couldn't believe this. He actually *wanted* this for her. Jade sat, dejected and betrayed. Timothy held her hand and she stared blankly at the rug. All she could see were Spencer's dark blue eyes as he'd laughed and turned away from her.

Jade squeezed her father's hand, pressing her lips together as she kept her focus on the floor. Her thoughts buzzed in her head, but one made itself heard above the noise.

I've moved on.

In the past seven years, Jade had had time to recover. She still thought of Spencer, wondering how he was and what he was doing, but she always stopped herself before it went too far. She could agree to this for now, if only to ease her father's mind. She could come up with a way out later.

"All right, Dad," she said, forcing the words from her throat with a smile. "I trust you."

* * * *

It had been worth it at the time to see her father's relieved expressions. Now, four days later in the early morning of July fifth, as she stood in her small Dallas apartment with all of her belongings packed away in brown boxes, Jade wasn't so sure. She had expected to be moving to New York in September and running the company from Alexander International. As she grabbed a black marker to scribble one last label on a box, reality began punching her in the gut. Paige Montgomery, Jade's best friend and the closest thing she'd had to a sister since middle school, put the tape down next to her. Paige surveyed the living room with her hands on her hips, looking rather pleased with herself.

Sometimes Jade wondered how they had become friends and, aside from their fathers working together, she couldn't think of a single reason. They were complete opposites in nearly every way. Paige was a dreamy type, someone who needed to be constantly pulled out of the clouds. She was a tiny thing, always in wispy dresses and skirts and humming to herself. Today, it was a rainbow patchwork maxi dress that complemented Paige's tanned, freckled skin. Her naturally pretty face and hazel eyes didn't need makeup, and her dark blonde hair was cropped short in a pixie cut.

When compared side by side, she made Jade look severe. Always the practical one, Jade wore a smart white blouse tucked into khaki slacks with a belt and tennis shoes. Her long black hair was pulled back into a perfect ponytail and she wore no jewelry or other adornments. Instead of a purse, she carried a messenger bag for her phone, wallet, keys and laptop.

"Are you excited?" Paige asked, making it very clear with her bouncing that *she* was. Jade rolled her eyes and turned away.

"What is there to be excited about? You were there for the aftermath of what Spencer did. And now I'm expected to live with him and marry him and… Ugh!" Jade swiped the tape and marker off the box lid, making them clatter to the floor. This whole situation was so impossible.

"Come on. It's perfect! You'll arrive in New York, where Spencer Alexander will instantly fall in love with you, apologizing for the cad he once was. You will party and meet all sorts of celebrities and have the time of your life. Then, in September, you'll marry him and all your dreams will come true." Jade looked at her in disbelief. "Okay, maybe that was *my* fantasy after looking him up online last night. He looks completely different from who I remember."

"You're insane," Jade said, shaking her head. She still hadn't looked Spencer up and didn't intend to. She had one thing she wanted out of this trip, and it was *not* Spencer Alexander. Jade busied herself with double-checking her overnight bag.

"Have you seen Clint yet?" Paige asked. Clint Donne was another one of their best friends, and he was as different as they were. He was a proud Texan, always in jeans and cowboy boots. Sometimes he would even wear a cowboy hat. He was ruggedly handsome, and Jade had dated him in high school. But, after graduation, they'd come to terms with the fact that they wanted different things. Clint had wanted a simple life and Jade had wanted Spencer. In the end, they'd decided to remain friends.

"Not yet," she answered. "We're supposed to meet up before I leave." Just then, there was a knock at the door.

"I'll get it!" Paige sang as she skipped to the front door. Jade laughed. She would miss Paige. The door swung open to reveal her mother, who quickly enveloped Paige in a hug, then Jade. The older Jade grew, the more she realized that she looked just like Angela Saunders.

"What are you doing here?" Jade asked. "I mean, not that I'm not happy to see you, but I thought we were supposed to all meet up at the airport later."

Her mom's smile turned into something a bit more forced.

"I'm afraid there's been a change," she said. "Apparently the Alexanders have sent their private jet to get you." Beside her, Paige squealed, but Jade balked.

"That wasn't part of the plan," she said. "Mom, I had other things to do today."

"I know, honey." Her mother looked genuinely upset, too. "But they want you there as soon as possible. They've even sent a limo for you. It's waiting outside." She gently pushed a stray strand of hair behind Jade's ear.

Great, even my hair isn't cooperating today.

Her mother went on. "But we'll be right behind you, no later than the end of the month. Don't forget that we have to be there for the engagement party."

"And I'll be up in a week to help with wedding planning!" Paige interjected. Jade smiled at them, tears pricking her eyes. How could they talk about this all so casually? Still, she wouldn't be able to get through this without them. Jade decided she would cooperate for now. She had the rest of the month to plead her case and try to get out of this asinine arranged marriage. She had to fake it for the time being, if only for her parents' sake.

"Thanks, guys." Jade hugged them both in turn then grabbed her two suitcases and slung her messenger bag over her shoulder. As the trio made their way down the stairs of her apartment building, Jade gave her mother and Paige instructions on the boxes and furniture, asking her mom to tell her dad goodbye for her.

Outside, shining in the weak morning sunlight, was a long black limousine.

With a last round of goodbyes and hugs, Jade handed her suitcases over to the driver and slid into the back seat of the car. Though the Saunders were wealthy, they were more on the humble side compared to the Alexanders, and her family only used limos for special occasions. Jade liked the Alexanders well enough, but knowing who'd sent the limo and where she was going twisted her stomach into a knot.

The car began to accelerate, and Jade turned around to look out of the back window. Her mom and Paige were waving, and she noticed the rusty blue pickup truck that she would recognize anywhere. She almost asked the driver to stop but knew that traffic was too busy to allow it. Clint stepped out of the truck and stared after her. She gave a weak wave, even though he probably couldn't see her.

Chapter Two

July 5

Twenty minutes later, Jade looked out the window to see that they were at a private hangar rather than the airport. There on the tarmac was a black-and-gray jet with a single stripe of crimson running from nose to tail.

That must be my ride.

The driver opened the door for her and helped her out. A set of stairs was lowered from the jet and a single attendant stood at the top, a smile splitting her face. Jade blew out a sigh, whispered a quiet goodbye to Dallas, the only home she'd ever known, and started up the steps to her new life.

The attendant welcomed Jade warmly while her suitcases were secured in the cargo area. She offered to take her messenger bag, but Jade held on to the strap and politely declined. The laptop inside was not only her connection to her father's company, but her connection to everything...period.

The small plane was something Jade had only seen in movies. The cabin was spacious, but there were only four seats. She soon found the reason for that was because all the seats fully reclined and had large trays that folded down in front of them. There were many windows that filled the space with natural light, and a single gold plaque was fixed to a wall, claiming this plane as one of five jets owned by the Alexanders. Jade scoffed and rolled her eyes. There was no divider between the cabin and cockpit, but between the two areas sat a refreshment center.

The soft cream-colored leather of the thickly cushioned chair cradled her when she sat and, after having spent more than half the night packing, Jade was sure she could sleep the entire four-hour ride away. All it would take was the push of a button… But she stopped herself. She couldn't get too comfortable in what she viewed as enemy territory. In no time, the pilot and copilot filed in and settled into their stations. The attendant, whose nametag read 'Katie', went over procedures and the emergency plan.

"Do you have any questions?" she asked cheerily. Jade shook her head. "Mister Alexander wants this trip to be as relaxing and safe for you as possible. Would you like any refreshments?" Again, Jade declined, ignoring the comment about Spencer. She looked past Katie to where she could see into the cockpit. The engines had already warmed up, and Jade watched the two men prepare for takeoff.

Jade stared out of her window as the world grew smaller below. Dallas was glittering as the city came to life with the rising sun and she felt a pang of longing for her hometown. *It won't be forever*, she told herself. *New York will* not *become my home*. In fact, should all go according to plan, she would be back before the end of

August. As soon as the seat belt light flicked off, Jade adjusted the wooden tray in front of her and pulled her laptop from her bag. She didn't intend on wasting any time.

"Excuse me?" Katie's voice called her attention. The attendant had that saccharine grin plastered on her face again. "Mister Alexander has asked me to make sure you spend this time relaxing. If you could please put your laptop—"

"I know you're just doing your job, Katie," Jade said, "but so am I. And, with all due respect to Mister Alexander, he does not get to dictate what I do with my own time." She turned her attention to her screen then closed her eyes with a sigh. "I'm sorry. I don't know where my manners went. I shouldn't have snapped at you, Katie."

The attendant offered Jade the first genuine smile she'd seen from the woman.

"I understand," Katie said. Her voice lowered. "I know about the conditions of your trip. It's a lot of pressure on you. If you'll please let me know if you need or want anything, I'll leave you to your work."

Katie relaxed back into her own seat and stared out of the window. Jade wasn't sure what to say after that. If Katie knew details about her trip, then did all Spencer's employees? What about the pilots? Jade's face heated at the mere thought. She couldn't live with herself if everyone she was going to come into contact with was aware of the unpleasant arrangement. And what was all of this about? Did Spencer really tell them not to let her work?

Jade decided to distract herself with her computer. She set up her hotspot and got to work. Most of the ride was taken up with marketing research, replying to emails and going over more spreadsheets than she could count. Though it was a bit stressful, it was the kind of stress that Jade was equipped to handle, and working like this made her feel more at ease than anything else she could think of. It wasn't long before Jade's thoughts began to wander and she begrudgingly opened a new tab on her browser.

A quick search yielded the information she needed, and she clicked on the first site. A picture of Spencer Alexander filled her screen. Jade couldn't help the way her heartbeat picked up while she scrutinized the man she was supposed to marry. Gone was the awkward, gawky teenager, replaced with a handsome grown man. He still had short, dark brown hair and ocean-blue eyes, but his expression was focused. Thick eyebrows drawn together made him seem determined and ready for anything, and his lips — the lips that used to send her imagination into overdrive — were set in a line, not smiling like she remembered. He looked professional, more a serious businessman than the fun-loving boy he'd been the last time she'd seen him. Jade continued down the page to his biography.

The story was familiar, similar to her own with a very different ending. Spencer was the son of her father's family friend and self-starter Carlton Alexander. Both Carlton and Timothy had built their empires from next-to-nothing, but Carlton had eventually moved to the big city. Spencer had gone to college, earning a business degree and training with his father so that he could run Alexander International, a company with many different projects that spotlighted clean energy. He would be taking over AI in October at the age of twenty-eight, making him the highest-valued CEO under thirty — or so Jade read.

From what Timothy had told Jade, Spencer had introduced a project that would produce wind turbines for not only America, but also for several third-world countries, providing much-needed free energy to more people than ever before. Though the idea had been Spencer's, it had been his father who had recommended Saunders' Metalwork to take over production. Since then, it had gone from contracting SM, to flat-out buying the company. Jade still wasn't happy about it, but it hadn't been her decision.

A bit below the bio were links to websites of the charities Spencer had started. He had always been kind and generous, but Jade couldn't help but wonder if all this charity work was for show. She closed out of the page, somehow finding new motivation to work. She supposed any questions she had would be answered by the man himself in due time.

Sooner than expected, Katie announced that they were about to land, and Jade put her things away. She was beginning to grow anxious. What if this was worse than she thought? What if he had more power over her future than she'd been led to believe? What if seeing him again was more than she could handle? Jade watched the grass and asphalt rise to meet them as the plane landed smoothly and began to slow down.

Jade had hoped the skies would be as sunny as Texas' had been, but she had been able to tell from about an hour out that it would be gray and cloudy, ready to rain at any moment. Katie escorted Jade out of the plane to where yet another sleek black limousine waited for her, then she wished Jade luck before she set off across the tarmac. Once again, they were at a private hangar, probably property of Carlton Alexander. Jade searched the horizon and immediately made out the iconic Manhattan skyline. They were a good way off and it would be a long trip into the city.

"Miss Saunders?"

Jade turned to the short man wearing a suit and cap as he gestured to the open limo door. She hoped that the next few weeks wouldn't be like this. Jade wasn't used to being waited on in such a manner, and frankly, it made her uncomfortable.

Jade had been right about the lengthy trip into the city. She spent most of it thinking and watching the grass and trees fade into small communities — and eventually into smaller buildings. Looking at it now, it wasn't that different from Dallas. Honestly, it wasn't that impressive. Or perhaps Jade's sour mood and indifference to the concrete jungle she would call home for the next two months was due to fact that the next time she stepped out of this car, she would be standing in front of Spencer Alexander.

The limousine rolled to a stop in front of a towering skyscraper. Jade peered up, craning her neck to see how high it actually was, but the very top was lost somewhere in the heavy clouds that had overtaken the sky. Little dots of rain speckled her window. Jade thanked the driver and let him know that she could manage from there.

"It's no trouble, Miss Saunders," he said as he hopped out of the car. "Besides, I have my orders." He opened the door for her, making sure she was safely on the sidewalk before circling around to the trunk. He unloaded her luggage and Jade hurried to grab the handles of her suitcases and made sure her bag was strapped around her body.

"I can't thank you enough," she said before he could protest. "I really can take it from here." The older man gave an understanding nod and wished her a good day. Jade blew out a breath as the limo pulled away.

She turned back to the sidewalk, but her foot caught on the curb. She cursed as her cases tumbled onto their sides behind her, and she braced herself as much as she could for the impact that never came. Instead, a pair of strong arms scooped her up effortlessly and righted her. Before she could apologize or even express her gratitude, she was floored to discover that her first act in Manhattan was falling directly into the arms of the one person she did not want to see.

Spencer Alexander still had his hands on her sides, and Jade's first observation was that the picture on his website did not do him justice. His deep-blue eyes weren't cold or severe, but sparkled with compassion and a sincerity that warmed her. The faint scar he'd received when he was twelve and had fallen from her tree house still sat just above his left eyebrow. A slight shadow was present on his strong jawline and she doubted it ever went completely away. That was all it took for her feelings to come flooding back. Everything she had suppressed for the last seven years was as fresh in her mind as if it had never left. *Oh, God,* she thought, *there's no way I can still be in love with this man.*

The corners of his lips were tugging up into a smile, and that was when she grasped that he was laughing at her. Well, not laughing exactly, but there was a definitely a chuckle. She dismissed any love-related thoughts and blamed them all on nostalgia.

I am not still in love with Spencer Alexander.

"I'm fine, thank you," Jade mumbled, taking a step back to glare at him. He was wearing a fitted black designer suit with a white shirt and silver tie. He was immaculate, with his dark hair parted on the side, a single wave of his bangs falling onto his forehead. *Dammit,* Jade thought, *why does he have to be so attractive?*

"It's good to see you again, Jade," he said, sounding as though he genuinely meant it. His voice was a buttery baritone, the kind only found in leading men or professional voice actors. Jade took her time straightening her suitcases, all the while refusing to give in to his charms.

"Likewise," she replied shortly. She had to push away thoughts of the last time she'd seen him, back when he'd broken her heart. How did her parents expect this to work? *Because you never told them the whole story.* "Listen, Mr. Alexander—"

"Spencer," he interjected. "Come on, Jade. Please don't act this way."

"Mr. Alexander," she emphasized, visibly annoyed with him already, "I'm here for my parents. I do not intend to marry you, but I *do* intend to fight for my promised job. I have agreed to spend time with you and do my work, but let's be clear right now... That is *all* that will be happening. There will be nothing further than conversation every now and again."

Spencer lowered his head and tucked his hands into his pockets.

"Sounds good to me," he said. Jade raised an eyebrow. "As long as you give me a chance to redeem myself for...everything that happened. I know you still hold it against me, and I don't blame you, but a lot has changed in the past few years."

Embarrassment set the tips of her ears on fire at the mere mention of it.

"I understand," she said. "I suppose, given the circumstances, I can attempt to be a little more polite...Spencer."

"Let's get inside before we get soaked," he said, not bothering to hide his grin. It was in that moment that the rain started to fall in earnest. He took one hand out of his pocket and offered it to her. "Would you at least allow me to escort you?" Jade nodded but didn't take his hand. She couldn't do that yet. She collected her things and swept past him toward the building's entrance.

"May I help you with those?" Spencer asked, a note of amusement in his voice.

"No, thank you," Jade said, tightening her grip on the handles as she rolled the suitcases up the ramp. It was a childish thing to do, but she just couldn't help herself.

The first level was all shiny marble floors and gleaming metal columns. It was as she had expected, down to the golden 'AI' logo against the far wall. There were only a handful of employees in this area, including the receptionist and security guards. She didn't get to examine the room in more detail before Spencer came behind her and ushered her between the open elevator doors. It was then that his earlier words sank in.

"I'm confused," Jade said after he pressed the very top button — the ninetieth floor. "I thought I was going to your parents' house. Are we touring your building first?" Spencer smirked and ran a hand through his damp hair, managing only to mess it up in the process.

"Yes, about that…" He sucked in a breath through his teeth. "There has been a change in plans."

"Why is that all I've heard today?" Jade asked, mostly to herself.

"I truly am sorry, but instead of my parents' house, you'll be staying in the penthouse of this building."

Oh. Well, that will make things easier. She wouldn't have to be under the pressure of being a guest of the Alexanders and she would have her own space. And, since she would be working here, it would be nothing short of convenient.

Spencer had apparently caught on to her relief and grinned wickedly before adding, "To be clear... You'll be staying with me in my home."

Chapter Three

"Hold on… What?" Jade fixed her gaze on the man next to her. She had spent the entire day doing as she had been told and adapting to the Alexanders' changes, but this was unacceptable. This crossed the line. She refused to live with the person who was currently reveling in her discomfort, openly smirking at the entire situation. Was her entire existence a joke to Spencer? Jade swallowed hard. It occurred to her that this marriage nonsense might be some elaborate prank, but she doubted that Spencer would involve their parents in such a thing. He was an asshole, not a sociopath.

"My parents will be leaving for a small vacation in a couple of days and they didn't want you to be alone," Spencer explained. To his credit, he was trying to bite back the smile. "It also gives us a chance to better reacquaint ourselves. I barely recognize you anymore." Jade crossed her arms and huffed. She wished she could disappear or, better yet, go back in time and change everything with Spencer.

It had been a hot summer day in Texas. If Jade thought hard enough, she could still feel that dry heat seeping into her skin. She could still see Spencer, just beginning to fill out and come into his own. She had graduated from high school that spring and was feeling very grown up. Her heart had thudded in her chest in anticipation of what she was about to do, sweat beading along her forehead.

Jade looked over at Spencer, here in the air-conditioned elevator. There was no way she could do this. Resentment she'd been burying for the past seven years was clawing its way to the surface. The walls were closing in on her and the buttons on the panel were lighting far too slowly as they dragged her higher up the building.

"First you force me to marry you, then you force me to move in with you," Jade said. She was seeing red. Her life had been turned upside down in a matter of days, and now it seemed that no matter how hard she tried to adapt to the situations being thrust at her, she wouldn't get any of it back. "You know what? It's fine. I'll keep to myself and I expect you to do the same." The lights were nearing the top of the panel.

"Listen, Jade," Spencer started in a much lower voice than he had used thus far. He turned to her. His height and the enclosed space made Jade hold her breath. She hadn't noticed how tall he'd become. "I meant what I said, and I *am* sorry. I understand that this whole thing must be exasperating for you. It is for me, too. So, let's get some facts straight.

"First of all, I *did* not and *am* not forcing you to do anything. None of this was up to me. It was all our parents. Secondly, while I do plan on making everything up to you, I'm not going to spend every single day that I'm around you apologizing. I know that you couldn't care less about our arrangement, but there is too much at stake here for both of us and we can't get anywhere unless we work together. So I would appreciate a little effort on your part, if it's not too much trouble."

The elevator doors slid open and Spencer motioned for her to step out before him. Jade, still reeling from the unexpected lecture and not wanting to admit that he was right, entered the penthouse with Spencer on her heels. It was a sleek, modern home — very beautiful, but lacking the cozy warmth she had grown up with. The layout was open, with floor-to-ceiling windows all around the main room and doors that led out to a balcony. The floor was white tile and the walls were ivory, which would have seemed cold if not for the dark wood and steel furniture and accents. There was a dining area and kitchen off the main room.

Spencer directed her up a wooden spiral staircase where he told her the bedrooms were. The second floor had a half-wall, which she could look over and see into the main room and kitchen. The room that had been made up for her had an identical decor to the rest of the home, but with touches of light blue here and there. She had the standard king-size bed, nightstand and wardrobe, and an office space set up in the corner. She even had her own private balcony. Her attention was pulled back to the desk, which had a large brown envelope resting on it.

"I'm right down the hall," Spencer said. His voice had softened back to his usual tone since the elevator, and Jade felt a little guilty for how she had acted toward him. He had apologized. And he was right... This hadn't even been his idea. None of this was directly his fault. She was being a child about events that were no longer relevant. They were both adults now, both had moved on and it was ridiculous to hold on to an old grudge as strongly as she had.

"Thank you," she said, managing an even tone. There... She had taken the first step. Spencer nodded and smiled, parting his full lips to show white teeth in a way that seemed almost shy or nervous. Some of the hostility she'd held toward Spencer began to dissolve. *Damn it all, how can he still have that effect on me?*

"Take your time getting settled," he said, turning to leave. "I'll be late, so if you need anything, there's a number on the fridge you can call — or you can ask Bryce once he gets here." He was already halfway down the stairs before she could say anything else, and she rushed after him.

"Wait! Whose number is it?" she shouted down the stairs. "Yours? And when will Bryce be here?" Spencer was already in the elevator and gave her an exaggerated shrug before the doors closed. Jade blew out an irritated breath. If he was going to be like this all the time, she didn't know how the next few weeks would work.

* * * *

An hour later, Jade was sprawled on her new king-sized bed, listening as the deluge outside pounded the windows. It hadn't taken her long to unpack — clothes and shoes went in the wardrobe, messenger bag on the desk and empty suitcases under the bed. She had explored a little and found that she had her own private bathroom attached, already stocked with her favorite soaps and products. She didn't know whether to be creeped out or impressed when she set her toiletry bag on the counter. Honestly, no matter what Spencer had done to make her comfortable, this space seemed more like a hotel to her. It was easier to think of it that way, so she didn't mind.

Jade suddenly sat straight, gazing at the brown envelope that had been nagging at her brain. She had some idea what was inside but had been so afraid of being right that she couldn't bring herself to touch it. She'd have to check at some point, though, and there was no time like the present. Jade stood and snatched it from the desk before ripping it open.

Its contents were what she'd expected—a copy of the Saunders' company policy and a list of employees who would be staying with the company, along with some other contracts and documents. The last thing was a single sheet of paper. Jade's stomach dropped. In her hands was the contract outlining the requirements of her marriage to Spencer. It was highly detailed, going so far as to mention children. Two lines sat at the bottom awaiting both her and Spencer's signatures. Jade couldn't look at it anymore and balled the paper up, tossing it into the waste bin. She knew there were likely more copies, but that didn't mean it wasn't satisfying to throw that one away.

Jade needed air. She needed to get out of the room. She grabbed her coat from the wardrobe and her wallet and started down the stairs. She hadn't eaten yet, so maybe she could grab a taxi and find a nice, quiet restaurant, far away from this building. Before she could reach the elevator, the doors parted and a man carrying a pizza looked at her expectantly. Jade froze, temporarily wondering if Spencer had his home bugged. She involuntary cut her eyes to the corners of the ceiling.

"Hey, Dave," a familiar voice spoke from behind her. Jade turned, expecting to confront Spencer, but had to catch herself. The person approaching her was a younger, more vibrant version of Spencer, with playful blue eyes and messy hair. He was dressed in a fashionably wrinkled white button-down and beat-up classic Converse, his hands shoved into the pockets of black jeans. He gave Jade a lopsided grin as he passed 'Dave' a few bills and took the pizza.

"Later, Bryce," Dave said before he left. Jade had to do a double-take. This was Bryce? This was the eleven-year-old menace who would chase her around the yard, pretending to be a cowboy or an alien or whatever had held his interest that week? Bryce had lost the baby fat and turned into a young man out of nowhere. Jade couldn't hardly believe it.

"Jade," he said, wrapping his arm around her while still clutching the pizza box.

"Jesus, Bryce, you've grown." She laughed. How was he so much taller than her?

"I didn't know if you'd remember me. Spence hasn't shut up about you for nearly a week. Wanna slice of pizza?" He took the pie to the kitchen, set it on the counter then retrieved two plates from a cabinet. Jade knocked herself from her stupor. She would love to have lunch with Bryce! Jade took off her coat, put down her purse then sat at the bar while the younger Alexander served her.

"Thank you," Jade said before digging in. She hadn't realized how hungry she was until the piping hot cheese and sauce hit her tongue. She had never tasted pizza quite like this and feared she never would again. Jade began to eat in earnest, and Bryce went ahead and slid another slice onto her plate.

"So," he started, "been a while, huh?" Jade nodded, her mouth full. "I'm happy to see you again, but you picked a bad day to come to New York. It's supposed to be raining into tomorrow night."

"I didn't pick the day," Jade said as she finished the first slice. *I didn't really pick anything.* Jade shoved the bitterness down with a fresh bite of pizza and continued. "Plus, I don't mind the rain." She was thinking a bit more clearly now that she had something in her stomach, and a key sentence from their introductions struck her. "So, what was that earlier? Spencer was talking about me?"

"Oh, yeah," Bryce said with a devious grin that told her he was eager to embarrass his brother. "He was super nervous this morning. He was acting like a girl, changing clothes and styling his hair. *'Does this look okay? Should I change my tie?'* It was great." Jade felt even more guilty about how she'd acted. She definitely owed Spencer an apology. *But you don't owe him any more than that,* she was quick to remind herself.

"So, tell me what you've been up to. Do you live here, too?" Jade needed the subject change, and she wanted to catch up with the boy she used to babysit. He finished his own bite before answering.

"No, I still live with my parents," he said. "They live just outside the city. But now that I'm out of school, I visit Spence all the time. You could say I'm here today for moral support." He followed his words with a sly smile and Jade knew what that meant. Odds were good that Bryce had spent the morning telling Spencer how awful he looked and handing out plenty of bad advice.

Over lunch, Jade learned more about who the Alexander brothers had become. Spencer was addicted to his job, getting up before the sun and usually returning home near midnight. Jade could relate to that. Maybe they did have more in common than she'd thought. She also found out more about what Bryce had been up to. Now that he was eighteen and a legal adult, Bryce was determined not to live in Spencer's shadow.

He would be going to college the next year and had dreams of taking over the European branch of Alexander International when he was done.

"That's pretty noble," Jade said when he'd told her of his plans. "Most siblings prefer the 'trust-fund baby' lifestyle. That's what I always tagged you as, anyway."

"Tried it. Not my thing," he said with a laugh. They finished the whole pizza together, then Jade helped him clean up the dishes before he told her he should probably be heading home. "It was good to see you, Jade," he said. "And don't let Spencer fool you. He hated what happened between you two." He gave her one more hug before leaving. She admired Bryce's attitude and was proud of who he'd become.

She looked around the now-empty apartment, which seemed too big for her. Jade hurried up the stairs, back to her room and shut the door. Her bedroom was smaller, and the silence didn't echo around her.

Jade took the crumpled contract from the waste bin and flattened it over the desk. Turning on the lamp, she read through the words a dozen times. Spencer had been right. Everything had been charted out by their parents, so he'd had no say. However, this was marked as a draft and that gave her hope. She read through one more time, trying to find a way around the rules that were set out. The only way she would be able to keep full control of Saunders Metalwork was to either marry Spencer, strike a new deal with him or to void the purchase altogether.

But, she argued with herself, *if you don't sell to AI, then your parents don't get their golden parachute, do they? And everything Dad has worked hard to build might be ruined.* It only took one broken deal to destroy a business' reputation. Jade laughed at the corner she was trapped in. Either way, she was going to have to try to get along with Spencer.

Chapter Four

July 6

One thing about rain... It made Jade sleep like a baby. That, combined with the lack of rest and the memory-foam mattress, caused Jade to sleep in until nearly nine, a far cry from her usual six a.m. wake-up. She sat up and stretched, feeling a kind of energy she had been severely lacking since Timothy had given her the 'big news'. She lowered her feet to the floor, but the cold tile she expected wasn't cold at all.

"Of course, he has heated floors," Jade said, rolling her eyes. But she wouldn't complain too much about the comfortable warmth she was able to walk across. Outside, the sky was foggy and rain still streamed down the windows, making it difficult to make out more than the peaks of buildings high enough to rise over the mist. Jade felt bad for those stuck on the ground, especially the ones who couldn't hail a taxi.

She was on her way to the bathroom when she heard unfamiliar mumbling outside the door. She slipped on her robe and cinched it tight before stepping out. As she made her way downstairs, she recognized the voices mixed with the sounds of hurried steps and dishes clattering against each other.

The living room had been completely rearranged to make room for tables and cushioned chairs, platters for finger foods, empty glasses and vases of flowers. And there, picking at a tray of sandwiches, was Bryce. Jade hurried over to him.

"Hey, I was just about to come get you," he said around a mouthful of ham.

"What is all this?" Jade asked, glancing around at the strangers.

"It's your welcome party," Bryce told her, throwing an arm around her shoulders and pulling her close. "It officially starts at eleven, so you'd better start getting ready."

"Why didn't anyone tell me?"

"Maybe Spencer wanted to surprise you — or maybe you didn't give him a chance to tell you." Jade nervously tucked a strand of hair behind her ear. "Probably it's just supposed to be a surprise, though." Bryce poked her side and she ducked out from under his arm with a giggle.

"That's not nice," she scolded.

"Go get dressed," he said. "You don't want to be late to your own party, do you?"

Jade laughed, taking the stairs two at a time and freezing at the landing. She stared at Spencer's door, wondering briefly if he was in there. She shook the thought from her mind and returned to her room.

The first thing she did was grab a dress from the wardrobe, and thank God she had thought to pack one at all. Jade showered quickly then blow-dried her hair.

The dress was one her mother had bought her after she'd graduated. It was bright red, with sleeves that fell off the shoulders and came to her elbows. The knee-length dress was made of linen, but had a red-lace overlay that gave it a more casual look.

Jade added a touch of makeup, a bit of liner and shadow around her eyes and red lipstick to match her dress, then brushed her hair to fall in waves down her back. After putting simple diamond studs in her ears and slipping on her Louboutin Bianca heels, she was ready to go. It was close to eleven when Jade took a deep breath and started down the spiral staircase.

She didn't expect the reaction she got. The main room was crowded with dozens of people who all went quiet as they fixed their eyes on her. She searched the room for familiar faces and eventually spotted Bryce, who was busy chatting with a redheaded woman she didn't know. Another scan of the room and she found Spencer. Her steps slowed.

Spencer was standing next to an older couple whom she recognized as his parents, with a drink in one hand and his gaze concentrated only on her. It was then that time picked back up and Jade was at the bottom of the stairs, surrounded by people who were introducing themselves and asking her questions. It was a lot at once, but Jade had been in situations like this before and knew how to handle it.

She wove her way through the masses, answering what she could and memorizing names and faces, noting the ones who were relatives and who were business associates. They were all executives and employees. None seemed to be simply friends. Did Spencer even have friends anymore? Jade was a workaholic, too, but at least she had Paige and Clint.

Finally, she arrived at the kitchen counter-turned-bar where all the Alexander family had congregated. She joined Carlton and Victoria, Spencer's parents. Carlton was a man in his mid-fifties, with salt-and-pepper hair and a dazzling smile. Victoria was everything a lady should be, with a lovely black dress and diamond jewelry, but there was an underlying playfulness in her mannerisms. It was plain that any mischievousness that came from Bryce or Spencer had been passed down from Victoria.

They were very polite to her and asked all sorts of questions, especially about how her parents were doing and how her travel had been, before welcoming her to their family. Jade's smile began to falter, but she quickly recovered and thanked the couple for their hospitality. They went off to mingle, leaving Jade alone with Spencer and Bryce.

The youngest Alexander readily filled the silence that would have swallowed them whole by telling Jade about their trip. He was going with his parents to Italy the next day and they wouldn't be back for about a week. Jade was genuinely excited for him and the experience he would gain. But it didn't take very long for Bryce to finish share his news and it took even less time for him to become distracted and wander off.

"You look lovely," Spencer said almost as soon as Bryce was out of earshot. Jade turned to him, where he was staring down at his untouched drink, swirling the contents around. "I'm sorry. I wanted to say something earlier, but I wasn't sure how to work it in." He looked up at her through long lashes and smiled.

"You're not half bad yourself," Jade said with a chuckle. She wanted to only half-mean it, but he did look very handsome, with a blue button-down that matched his eyes perfectly. The top two buttons of his shirt were open to show his collarbone, and the sleeves were casually rolled up. The shirt was tucked into black slacks and paired with black shoes. His hair was even a little unkempt, which Jade found endearing. *Damn it. He's not supposed to be endearing.* Spencer took a sip from his glass before setting it down on the counter.

"Come on," he said as he took her hand. "There are some people I want you to meet." Jade pulled her hand from his, tucking her hair behind her ear awkwardly. Spencer paused for a moment but didn't look back. Jade noticed how gentle his grip had been, almost hesitant, and how warm his skin had been against hers. She couldn't afford any contact right now. He worked his way through the crowd with Jade until he stopped in front of a woman. She was beautiful, with fierce blue eyes and long, dark hair pulled back in a ponytail. Her dress was professional, but not overly so. It was tight and black and hugged her curves in all the right ways, and Jade felt a sharp twinge of jealousy. The woman turned to study Jade through her glasses, barely acknowledging Spencer.

"Jade, I'd like you to meet Kindall Armstead," Spencer said. Kindall's face suddenly broke into a friendly smile as she shook Jade's hand. "She's our exclusive event coordinator at AI, and she is currently in charge of our engagement party and wedding." Jade tensed at the mention of the wedding, and regret began to flood into her. *I should have just stayed in bed.*

"Such a pleasure," Kindall said with a sweet drawl. She was definitely not from Texas, but was obviously from the Deep South. "Spencer has told me all about you and I can't wait to start working with you. I already have some ideas for the engagement party if you'd like to hear them." Her accent made Jade feel more at home and she relaxed. The two women talked for a bit, but Jade tried her best to avoid discussing the upcoming nuptials. *Never going to happen*, she told herself. They briefly went over their schedules and Kindall made plans to for them to meet on the fourteenth to start preparations. Jade forced a smile.

After Kindall, Spencer introduced Jade to the board of directors at AI. They were all courteous and told her how much they looked forward to working with her in the future. As a board member herself, Jade was also excited about that.

"What about her?" Jade asked, as Spencer led her back to the bar. It was the woman Bryce had been talking to earlier and was currently with. She didn't quite fit in with the rest of them. While everyone else wore neutral suits or borderline-evening wear, she wore a floor-length turquoise and gold dress that looked as if it had come straight off the runway. Her fiery-red hair was piled high on her head and she was laughing a little too hard at something Bryce had said. The woman caught Jade's eye for only a split second before Spencer tugged her away.

"She's an acquaintance," Spencer said curtly. "Just a friend of the family who has nothing to do with AI." Still, the woman stuck with Jade. Whoever she was, Spencer wasn't a fan and didn't want Jade to be either. She assumed it was a business deal gone sour — or that the fashionista had once been involved with one of the Alexander brothers. Either way, Jade knew that this wasn't the time to push, and she honestly didn't have the will to do so. They finally reached the kitchen and sat down on bar stools, away from the buzzing groups that had developed. Silence hung thick between them.

"Did you know that my parents were matched through an arranged marriage?" Spencer asked out of nowhere. Jade faced him and shook her head. She had an idea where he was going with this. "They were. And now, look at them. They're madly in love." He directed her attention to the pair, who were deep in conversation with another couple. Carlton wrapped an arm around Victoria's waist and smiled down at her proudly.

"What's your point with all this?" Jade asked, her gaze drifting back to Spencer.

"My point is that I know you're unhappy with this situation," he said. "It's not ideal for me, either. But happiness and even love are possibilities for us. And we have a past together, more than they did. We grew up together, Jade. I'm not saying it won't take time, but—"

Jade let out a laugh of disbelief.

"Did you really think this would work?" she asked as she crossed her arms. Spencer blinked with surprise. "Spencer, this isn't only about the marriage. It's about *everything*. You broke my heart with no explanation and now you expect me to forget about it, forgive you and *marry* you. Are you *that* delusional?" A sharp pain gripped her chest and she tightened her arms. She wouldn't give him the satisfaction of seeing her hurt, only angry.

"When are you going to get it through your head that we are in this together?" he asked, surprise giving way to apparent irritation. He lowered his voice, obviously not wanting to cause a scene. "I am trying everything to make this work, Jade. This whole thing is something our parents cooked up and I thought that it might not be a bad idea. We could certainly do worse.

And let me remind you that I was not even there when the papers were drawn up. Why do you think I gave you those copies?"

"It seemed like a scare tactic at the time," Jade seethed. "Don't you get it? I can't trust you. I *don't* trust you."

"I gave you those papers so you would have a say, Jade." He seemed more tired than annoyed. "I can't believe this. What type of person do you think I am?"

"I think you're the kind of person who would leave a young girl crushed and never even explain yourself. Also, if you would have taken the time to talk to me about this deal yesterday — which is why I'm here, by the way — I wouldn't have to assume things all the time." Jade slapped her hand on the white marble counter, causing a few heads to turn their direction. Spencer raised an eyebrow at her. He stood and leaned over close enough for her to smell his Clive Christian cologne, the scent making her head swirl a little.

"Well, Miss Saunders, I promise you that I will do everything I can to help with whatever it is you need. If it's an explanation you want, I'll give you one when you stop acting so childish." His voice dropped and he angled even closer, his lips near pressing against the shell of her ear. "It would be wise to keep in mind that I worked my ass off to get to where I am today and I will *not* allow you to jeopardize my position at this company. No. Matter. What." With that, he strode off, disappearing into the crowd. Jade took several breaths to calm her heart, which was hammering in her chest.

Chapter Five

July 7

Jade opened her eyes promptly at seven, slapping her alarm clock to shut the annoying thing up. Light was pouring into her room, so she lifted the covers over her head to block it out. She had hardly slept at all the previous night. She'd kept tossing and turning, her mind and body restless with the day's events. Spencer had disappeared after the party, so they'd never resolved their little spat, and that bugged her. Was she being too hard on him? He did deserve it, right? Jade sighed. She would have to apologize to Spencer before he left for work.

Figuring she might as well start her day, Jade threw back the blankets and padded across the room to her bathroom. She took full advantage of the cavernous waterfall shower, idling in the steamy bliss it offered. When she got out, she brushed her teeth and twisted her hair up in a messy bun. She threw on a pair of gray pants and a sleeveless white blouse, deciding against shoes for the day. She didn't have anything planned, and there was no work to occupy her yet, so she wasn't sure what she would be doing with the rest of the time she'd been given to settle in.

As soon as Jade stepped out of her room, she could hear voices from the floor below and recognized one of them as Spencer's. *Perfect*, she thought. Then the other voice registered as Carlton Alexander. Knowing full well that what she was about to do was wrong, Jade snuck over to the half-wall that overlooked the living room, sliding her socked feet across the tile so as to not make a sound. Below her, she could see Carlton as he relaxed in one of the armchairs while Spencer paced before him.

"You need some stability in your life other than work," the older man was saying. It was already eerily similar to talks Jade had had with her own father. "I like Jade — always have — and I think you'll be good for each other. Don't forget that we started out as a family-owned business and that is a value I want to uphold."

"She has no interest in me, Dad," Spencer said, throwing his hands in the air before resting them on his hips. "I've tried. You don't know how many times I've thought about calling her over the years. And you weren't there that summer. You don't know how much I hurt her. I didn't mean to… It's complicated. Anyway, I'm still trying to earn my spot in your chair, and I can't be bothered with all of this."

"Son, you have to give it a shot. I know it doesn't seem important now, but family is the number one thing in this life." Carlton was being extremely patient, speaking in calm tones. Still, she knew the pressure he was putting on his son, however unintentional. "I'm not worried about you doing well with the company. I'm worried about you being alone for the rest of your life. You only talk to us, and even then, it's usually about work." He lowered his voice even more. "And if it's proving yourself that worries you, this could help. If you get married, the shareholders will see you as someone dependable, someone who can commit."

"Is it wrong to have career goals now?" Spencer began to pace, ignoring his father's last comment while leaving Jade's line of sight. She didn't dare try to move closer out of fear of being spotted. "And I don't want Jade for the shareholders, Dad. I just want Jade, and she won't even give me a chance." He sounded so sad, and yet Jade felt her heart skip.

He *wanted* her. *What did he say about not meaning to hurt me?*

"Give her time," Carlton said. "You've had more time to process everything, and she hasn't. You need to give her space and she'll adjust. Also, an apology wouldn't hurt."

"I think it would be easier if she would hear me out, though," Spencer said. "I need to explain myself. I had my chance yesterday, and I blew it. If we could get everything out in the open, I wouldn't have all this guilt eating away at me." Jade could hardly believe what she was hearing. He was serious. He wanted this to work and it meant more to him than business.

"We'll see," was all Carlton said. "You two have until next month to figure things out. When you're ready, we and the Saunders will sit down to finalize everything. Until then, how about you take some time off and get to know this new Jade a little more?"

"I will soon." Spencer resumed his pacing. "Promise." Carlton sighed, pushing himself up from the chair.

"I'll leave that up to you, Spence," he mumbled. "Now, if you'll excuse me, I have a beautiful wife and a bratty teenager to take on vacation." Jade could hear the jovial way Carlton said this and smiled to herself. The current head of Alexander International was exactly how she remembered him. Spencer told his father goodbye as Carlton made his way to the elevator.

Before he was even halfway there, the reflective doors parted and out stepped the redheaded woman from the day before. Jade ducked down a little farther. The newcomer wore an award-winning grin and looked her own kind of professional in a lime-green pantsuit and stark white heels. Jade hated how the woman could get away with those looks without being a complete train wreck. She had to be a supermodel. The woman greeted Carlton with a hug, which he clearly tolerated and nothing more.

"It's so good to see you, Carl," she said in a simpering voice. "I wasn't expecting you to be here."

"Yes, well, I'm on my way out, Stacy." Carlton removed the woman's long limbs from around him and said a forced goodbye. Jade could tell this Stacy was an issue, from both Carlton's reaction and Spencer's bored expression. After the doors to the elevator closed behind Carlton, Stacy tossed her long hair over her shoulder and set her sights on Spencer.

"Sweetie, you didn't even say hello to me yesterday," she mewled, swaying her hips as she approached him. "Even Bryce was friendlier than you. I know your new friend saw me and you didn't bother to introduce us. So, what's the deal?" She was inches from Spencer now, her flawless, claw-like acrylic nails tracing spirals over his chest. Jealousy was beginning to creep through Jade. *Who does this person think she is?* It wasn't like Jade had any claim, but, well, didn't she? She still felt something for Spencer, and he'd told his father...what Carlton had wanted to hear?

"It's none of your business," Spencer said coolly. "What do you want, Stacy?" He swatted her hand away and she pouted.

"You know what I want," she said. Stacy reached up again to loosen Spencer's dark red tie. "I want the same thing I had last time." Then Jade's breath caught as Stacy rose up and kissed Spencer. That did it. Jade backed away from the balcony, pressing herself against the wall. Part of her wanted to run to her room and hide and the other wanted to go downstairs and show Stacy that she wasn't someone to mess with.

In the end, Jade decided not to go for the latter, but she made sure to slam her door shut so that it echoed through the apartment. She turned the lock and stood with her fingers in her hair, trying to process what she had witnessed. When Spencer and Carlton had been talking, there had been a spark of hope. She had learned that there might be something there that they could work out, that Spencer wasn't so bad after all. She had been ready to talk to him.

But what if it had all been a show? What if his whole tirade had been made up to appease Carlton and get him to back off? She knew the old Spencer would never have lied like that, but the new Spencer had told her yesterday that nothing would stand in the way of something he had worked so hard for.

This 'Stacy' had been all over him, but maybe it was all one-sided. Spencer certainly hadn't been thrilled by her proximity. Then again, she had been at Jade's welcome party, too, so the Alexanders definitely knew her. Then there was how familiar she had been with Carlton, even though he hadn't liked it. Had Stacy and Spencer been dating before this all began and now were hoping to continue their relationship, even though he was technically engaged?

That was ridiculous. Her mind was running away with her, like last time. She'd run away then without giving Spencer a chance to react. Why did she keep doing this around him? Jade's head began to pound as her thoughts raced and tangled, rendering any common sense useless. She began to search through her bag for some aspirin. Soon, there was a knock on the door.

"Jade?" Spencer's voice called. "Are you awake?"

"Yes," she answered, her voice quivering slightly. Damn, she wished it hadn't done that.

"Can I come in?"

"No, not right now," she said, fumbling for an excuse. "I-I'm not dressed yet." *Idiot. Let him in. No, don't let him in. Don't trust a word he says.*

"Okay, well…" He trailed off.

She could imagine him standing there with one hand on his hip and the other scrubbing his face. She wanted to let him in, but there was something holding her back.

"Are you all right?" He waited for her to respond.

"Yeah," she finally managed. "Like I said, I'm not dressed. You can go back to work. Don't worry about me." Jade wrung her hands, hoping that would be enough to make him leave. She had a lot to sort through.

A few seconds later, he spoke. "Okay. My number is still on the fridge, so if you need anything at all, call or text me, all right?"

"Yeah," was the most she could manage. She watched his shadow reflect on the tile below her door, hovering then leaving. Jade released her breath and popped the aspirin into her mouth, swallowing them dry. She knew the two of them would have to talk eventually, and she would let him explain everything the first chance he got, but she couldn't deal with it right now.

"Speaking of things I can't deal with," Jade muttered. Her phone had begun to ring in her pocket, its music-box tone filling the room. One look at the screen showed a number she didn't recognize. She swiped ignore and sat at the desk with her arms crossed on the surface. Her phone pinged, this time with a text from the unrecognized number.

Hi, it's Kindall! Got your number from Spence. Was wondering if you had time to talk?

That would be a no. How had Spencer even gotten her number? Jade ignored the message. Wedding planning was not something she was prepared for yet. She took her laptop from her bag and set up her workstation. Spencer had been considerate enough to fill the drawers of the desk with pens and paper, along with various other office supplies. She took the large brown envelope from inside her bag as well and set it next to her computer.

Jade booted up the device for the first time since she'd gotten there. It blinked to life, welcoming her back and displaying the time. The first thing Jade did was open her email, expecting the inbox to have piled up over the past two days. Nothing new had arrived since the plane ride. Jade resisted the urge to slam her fist against the desk. Her father must have cut her off from work for the time being. She knew he was trying to give her a break, but she would have a talk with him about that.

Jade clicked the icon to compose a new email for Paige. She apologized for not being in contact the past couple of days, then began to tell her everything. She told her about the flight, about the weather, about her new home and the party. She left out the conversation she'd overheard between Spencer and Carlton and how she had come to know this Stacy-person, though.

Jade read back through the letter, deciding to add Clint to the CC as well before hitting send. Once it was out there, Jade could breathe again. She quickly typed a new email, this time to her father. This one was a heavily watered-down summary of the last couple of days and a request that he start including her in the business once again. She made sure to emphasize how it would be more beneficial to her mental well-being if she were able to work, and after reviewing it, she sent it. Jade felt bad about the guilt trip but used the fact that she was upset to justify her actions.

"You need to stop being so petty," Jade scolded herself as she closed the laptop. "You'll keep being miserable if you hold on to it." She sat at the desk in absolute silence before coming to a few major decisions.

She would stop being uncooperative. More importantly, she would keep in mind that despite what may have happened in the past, Spencer was as chained to this as she was. Jade tossed the thought of Stacy from her head. For some reason, she hated to think about her touching him, hated to think about her kissing him. She took the contracts from the envelope and a red pen from the desk. She began to read and scratch notes in the margins.

I can fix this. I can fix all of it.

Chapter Six

Jade wasn't used to all this free time. Once she was done going through the documents Spencer had given her, her headache was back with a vengeance. She checked her phone, but neither Paige, Clint nor her father had replied to her emails. The thought crossed her mind to text them, but a keyboard had always suited her better. Jade couldn't wait until tomorrow, when she would hopefully begin working with AI. Seeing that it was nearly noon, she set the device down and stretched. Lunch would help ease the pain brewing behind her temples. Jade stood up and poked her head out of her room, but the apartment was deadly silent.

"Perfect." Jade grabbed the phone from her desk before descending the stairs and landing on the first floor. She was surprised when she saw that a dozen or so large boxes had been delivered. Jade stared at them in disbelief. Those were her boxes, the ones she had packed only a couple of days ago. They were supposed to be in storage, along with her furniture. She approached the stacks, checking that they were indeed her belongings. Her and Paige's handwriting neatly labeled the tops of each one.

"Mom…" she muttered under her breath. Honestly, she should have expected this. She should have put only Paige in charge of her belongings, rather than her mother. The whole point of packing was to give the *appearance* of moving. *Think positive*, she told herself. *Make an effort. It will be nice to have some of my own things again.* Jade left the boxes where they were and started toward the kitchen when something stopped her.

Jade inched closer to one of the windows. The rain and fog had hindered her view since her arrival, but now she could see everything in the clear sunlight. Hundreds of buildings stood below, stretching out to the water. The sky was cluttered with other skyscrapers, and Jade was in awe. Dallas was her heart, but she could get used to this.

Jade finally tore her gaze away from the spectacular sight and headed over to the kitchen. She had skipped breakfast for obvious reasons and her stomach was quick to remind her of it. On the stainless-steel fridge in bold font was Spencer's cell phone information and his schedule. *How considerate*, Jade thought, taking the paper down. It told her that Spencer would be out of the building for a lunch meeting and wouldn't be back until after two.

"Good to know." Jade tossed the page onto the counter and opened the fridge. Inside, it was stocked with everything imaginable. That seemed strange, as Jade hadn't once seen anyone cooking in here. Jade shrugged and pulled out eggs, bacon and butter.

Jade swiped through the apps on her phone and selected her music. An upbeat song bubbled from the tiny speaker and Jade set to work with a bounce in her step. She began frying the eggs in one of the many skillets she found and used another to start the bacon. A couple slices of bread went in the toaster, and she was back to check on her eggs. It felt familiar, dancing around the kitchen without rhythm while cooking. The strong perfume of sizzling bacon filled the apartment and Jade closed her eyes, imagining that she was home.

The toast popped up, startling her from her daydream, and she covered the slices with generous amounts of butter before plating the whole meal. She ate slowly, trying to kill as much time as she could. It was a foreign concept to Jade, but once she tried it, she found that taking things easy could be pleasant. For the first time since she couldn't remember when, she wasn't worrying about a deadline or staring at a screen. Time to herself was something else she could get used to.

Jade finished her meal and cleaned up the dishes. The page Spencer had left her caught her eye and she begrudgingly put the number into her phone, saving him under the name 'Confusion' for the time being. She figured, since she would be living here, it would be productive to have a look around.

The living room and kitchen were familiar to her, but there was a hall to the left of the elevator that held mysteries. The hallway was dark, and she couldn't find a light switch, but there was light from the other side, so it wasn't entirely necessary. At the end sat a lounge, very similar to the living room. The floor had a step down from the hall and, instead of tile, this room was outfitted with plush ivory carpet. The furniture was also cushier than the main room's—less formal in a way. A fireplace was set into the wall and a flat-screen TV hung over the mantle.

The sitting room had its own full bathroom and balcony, which Jade decided to step onto. The concrete was still damp from all the rain and Jade had to tiptoe over the bad spots. The breeze was warm but thin, and Jade could still smell the lingering rain, among other things. She filled her lungs with the fresh air, her very cells vibrating back to life. It was the first time she had been outside in two days. Jade heard a soft lapping sound next to her and saw that there was a full-sized swimming pool on the balcony.

"That's new," she said to herself before going back inside. Her room, as well as Spencer's, was upstairs. She was standing in front of his door, and the temptation rippled through her, but she stopped short of putting her hand on the knob. She wouldn't be that person who snooped into someone else's personal life, no matter how curious she was. Instead, she focused on the other two guest rooms. One was similar to hers, but barer and pure white. The other wasn't a bedroom at all, but an office.

Spencer must have turned one of the guest rooms into a home office. Jade found that strange, since he lived over his actual office, but she shrugged it off. If she had the space, wouldn't she have done the same? There was a desk in the center of the room facing the door. A small area set off to the side held a couch and coffee table, with a small bar behind.

The one thing that enraptured her, though, was the five-foot-tall portrait of Carlton Alexander that hung behind the desk. Carlton didn't quite look himself in the painting. His expression was stern, his forehead furrowed, and he was frowning slightly. Jade cocked her head to the side, trying to figure out if this was an official portrait or a joke for Spencer's sake.

"It makes me uncomfortable, too," Spencer said, his baritone voice startling Jade. "I know he meant it as a joke, but all I can hear when I look at it is his speech about how *'life doesn't give handouts, Spencer, and neither do I.'* But it keeps me focused, being constantly judged and all." Jade should have jumped ten feet in the air. Somehow though, Spencer's unexpected presence didn't scare her. She turned, finding him leaning his shoulder against the door frame with his hands clasped behind his back.

"Do you think it's funny to sneak up on people like that?" Jade teased. She berated herself for giving in so easily. *Aren't you still angry with him for some reason?*

"I sincerely apologize," he said, but any weight was lost in the playful grin that overtook his features. Jade took in Spencer's tall build. He wore the same black designer suit that she recognized from that morning. The top two buttons of his shirt were open and his burgundy tie was missing. The tie Stacy had taken off — or *might* have taken off.

Jade sensed the red-hot emotions stirring in her stomach as she suddenly remembered why she was angry with him. To keep from fuming, she had to remind herself that Spencer didn't belong to her and she still hadn't heard him out yet. The Stacy thing shouldn't upset her as much as it did, and she had no right to be jealous. *Yet.* Her thoughts must have shown on her face, though, because Spencer's smile faded and he straightened.

"My meeting was cut short," he said, offering an *excuse*, but not the one Jade was wishing for. "I wanted to check on you. I figured since I don't have any more work until this evening, we could sit down and talk?" Jade turned away to look at the portrait again. Even though she was no longer facing him, Jade could feel Spencer watching her.

"That's fine." She sighed, looking down at the desktop. Jade hadn't noticed it, but their contract was sitting on top of everything and it had familiar red words in Spencer's handwriting all over it. Jade closed her eyes and berated herself. *You said you would try. You have to meet him halfway.* "Should we go somewhere else or is here fine?"

"Name the place," Spencer said, his cheerfulness fully restored. "We don't have to be so stuffy, Jade. Try to relax a little. Whatever you want is what we'll do."

"I don't know. What do y'all do for fun around here?" Jade watched his lips quirk up in a smile and she cringed. She was trying to tamp down the southern accent, but it came out anyway. "Yes, hilarious. Seriously, what would you recommend?"

"I can think of a few things," he replied slowly, taking languid steps closer to her.

Jade backed up against the desk out of instinct, an eyebrow raised at him. *He couldn't seriously be insinuating — ?*

"I was thinking of a sightseeing trip, since you've never been to New York before." Jade's tensed muscles relaxed, likely visibly, and Spencer chuckled. "Why, Miss Saunders, what did you think I meant?"

"Nothing," she muttered, a blush rising to her cheeks. "I'll go grab my shoes." She rushed past him and once again got a whiff of his intoxicating cologne. *This is going to be an interesting trip.*

Jade ducked into her room and pulled her tennis shoes from the wardrobe. As she was tying them, she wondered what kind of tour he meant. Would he commandeer a bus or actually walk her around the streets? At the same time, she wondered when he would bring up Stacy, if at all. She knew that she couldn't be the one to do it. How could they have such a private conversation in a public place while sightseeing? When she got downstairs, Spencer was waiting by the elevator, behind the mountain of boxes.

"I'll have this sorted before we get back," he said, tapping a message out on the screen of his phone. Jade refused to look at the boxes.

"So, are you going to give me a tour of the city yourself?" Jade asked as Spencer put his phone away and called the elevator.

"Sort of," Spencer said with a shrug. "Trust me. It will be a good time."

"How long before you have to be back at work?" She was trying to get anything from him, any information that would give her a better idea of what to expect. He didn't reply and the elevator opened. When they got in, Spencer hit the button that would send them up. Jade didn't say anything.

Spencer's phone buzzed loudly in his pocket, alerting him to a message. He ignored it, but Jade couldn't. It began to buzz repeatedly, meaning that whoever had texted him was now trying to call. He pulled the phone from his pocket and turned it off, looking rather aggravated. The doors opened up to the roof and Spencer went ahead of her.

"You can take your calls if you need to," Jade said. She was a little uneasy being on top of a building this high. "I don't mind. Kindall was trying to reach me earlier. She might be trying you."

"It's not Kindall," Spencer said, coming to a stop a few steps away from the elevator. "And she can wait." He began to mutter angrily to himself. Jade wasn't sure who was attempting to reach Spencer, but she could certainly guess.

"Is it Stacy?" she asked, lowering her eyes to the ground. Spencer didn't miss a beat.

"Yes, it is." Spencer fiddled with his cuffs. "I take it you saw what happened this morning? I assumed you had." Jade nodded. "I am sorry about that. She was out of line and I let her know that in so many words before I sent her on her way. I've spent all morning avoiding her."

"Who is she?" Jade couldn't stop herself from asking. Sure, she was relieved to know that things hadn't gone any further than she'd seen, but she still wanted to know more.

"Just an old friend." Spencer raised a hand to his forehead, looking out over the skies. "No one you need to worry about."

"I am worried, though."

Spencer turned to her. There was something akin to hope in his deep blue eyes.

"I came here mostly for my parents, so if there's anything that could get in the way of this deal, like an old girlfriend, I need to know." The spark of hope fizzled but didn't quite disappear.

"I'll tell you what," he started. "I'll tell you everything you want to know on the ride, okay?"

"Ride?" Jade asked. Spencer pointed behind her. There, approaching them from the distance, was a helicopter. Jade looked down, only now noticing the bright orange and white paint carefully placed on the roof.

"I hope you enjoy flying."

Chapter Seven

Jade didn't mind flying. In fact, the helicopter that landed was one that she recognized. It was a Eurocopter, the exact same model Saunders Metalwork used in their business. Even though she had been in one more times than she could count and knew the safety regulations, Spencer held an arm out protectively in front of her to keep her far back from the landing aircraft. The spinning rotor blades were deafening and threatened to send Jade's hair flying in every direction.

The pilot gave Spencer a signal from inside the cockpit and he grabbed Jade's hand, urging her to the copter. Once inside, they strapped in and Spencer handed her a bulky set of headphones with a microphone, then slid a pair over his own head. Immediately, the abrasive machine's drones were canceled out by the foam ear pads.

"Can you hear me?" His voice echoed scratchily through the headset and Jade noticed that his hand remained on hers. Jade pulled away from him, leaning casually to look out of the window.

"Yes, I can hear you." Spencer didn't comment on her action and gave the pilot the go-ahead. Slowly, the copter began to rise. Even though Jade had a million burning questions to ask, she enjoyed the first bit of the ride. Since they were in Midtown, the copter took them further downtown, whizzing alongside the Empire State Building. As they passed the skyscraper, Jade kept cutting her eyes over to Spencer, who was looking out of his own window to the streets below.

Jade tried, but it was so hard to focus on the tour with this hanging over them. It was like he expected her to gawk at the scenes before her like some tourist, all the while forgetting the real reason behind this trip. As they were approaching downtown, Jade decided to speak.

"I remember how much you fought when your parents said they were moving to New York," she said into the mic. "It seems like it's grown on you." She needed something safe to start the conversation. Spencer faced her and nodded.

"I've visited a lot of other places, but I've never loved them as much as I do this city." He smiled at her. "Do you like it here?"

"It's beautiful so far," she answered honestly, glancing back outside. They were going over the dark waters of the Hudson River and Jade could see the spires of Trinity Church fast approaching, as well as One World Trade Center. To her other side, she watched glittering cars drive over the Brooklyn Bridge. The bridge was cramped with traffic, yet was somehow still awe-inspiring. "Um, what's your favorite color? I remember it used to be green."

"Really, Jade, I thought you would have grown into much more of a conversationalist," he said. "But I guess red, if I had to choose." Jade thought about how he'd watched her yesterday at the party in her red dress. But, no, that couldn't have had anything to do with his answer. *He used to like red, too, right?* She honestly couldn't recall. The copter was whipping over Battery Park, heading out to the ocean and Ellis Island.

"Hold on and I'll think of something better," she said, racking her brain for anything else to ask him. As much as she wanted to ask about Stacy, she couldn't be the one to bring it up again. That was his call. Thankfully, Spencer was well-versed in reading a person and put an end to her misery.

"I know you're waiting for an explanation." Spencer's clear voice spoke through the headphones. Jade didn't look at him, remaining silent. "I know that's what you want, and I already told you that I would give you answers. All you have to do is ask."

"All right." Jade glued her focus to the water below, avoiding his piercing stare at all costs. "Who is Stacy and what does she mean to you? And please be honest with me." She listened through the headset as Spencer exhaled loudly before beginning.

"Stacy Washington is a person who I was briefly involved with," he said. Jade turned back to look at him. "I've never been good at relationships, Jade. It's one thing that worries me about you and all...this."

He threw his hand in the air and Jade guessed that he was talking about more than Stacy. It could also explain the reason she had been rejected by him all those years ago.

Before she could dwell on it any further, he continued. "My last relationship went bad a couple of months ago and I made the mistake of going out and drinking way more than I should have. That's where Stacy came in.

"She took advantage of my inebriated state, and I won't lie to you, we slept together. It was one time, and I've regretted it ever since. Now she has it in her head that we're together. She's introduced herself to my family and colleagues and is using that to further her own status and the store she owns. She's some sort of fashion designer, and knowing an Alexander in such a way sounds good to a lot of labels." Spencer slid a hand through his hair in frustration. "I know all she wants is my money and influence, and she's trying whatever she can to get it."

"I'm sorry. I can't even imagine what that's like." Jade had only ever been with one man, Clint, but he had never tried to use her, even when he'd found out who her family was. Spencer must have had it harder than she'd thought.

"That's one reason I've been going along with this," Spencer admitted. "I know you don't *need* me. You don't need anything from me. You never have. And that means I can trust you more than I can trust anyone. I only wish you would trust me."

"I did need something from you, Spence," Jade said. "You were my first love. I needed you to take me seriously." She could see something on his face, something like shame or regret or a mix of the two. The helicopter was turning back, circling around the Statue of Liberty. If the mood in the copter hadn't been so grim, Jade would have been excited to see it this close, but she wasn't finished asking questions yet. She had the upper hand and she had to keep it.

"What did you do this morning?" Jade breathed into her mic. His answers now were more important than ever. "What did you do after Stacy kissed you?"

"Like I told you, I pushed her away," he said without hesitation. "Then after I heard your door shut, I told her to get out and that I never wanted to see her again. What did you think happened?"

Jade shrugged. She had assumed the worst, of course.

"Listen, Jade, because I'm only going to tell you this one time. I would never, *never* be unfaithful to you or anyone else. It's not in my nature. I know we don't even mean anything to each other right now, but I hope we can change that."

"Now you want to change things?" Jade scoffed. She'd heard him out, but part of her was still bitter and she didn't know how to move past that. "It's like you keep forgetting that you *broke my heart*, Spencer."

"I know, and I am sorry for that." Spencer's voice was near desperate and he repositioned himself, twisting in his seat so that he was entirely focused on her. "But I want a second chance. We're virtual strangers at this point, and we've been told that we have to be married soon. When my father told me about you, do you know how I felt?"

Jade shook her head, pure confusion clouding her mind. She truly wanted to believe him. Spencer raised his hand, brushing his fingers lightly on her cheek.

"Like I'd been given an opportunity to rectify the single biggest regret of my life. I never forgave myself for what I did to you. And when I found the courage to finally look you up, I saw that you had become an amazing, beautiful, inspiring woman, and you did it all without me." He was laughing now, and Jade couldn't help the rising urge to join him. She had missed him so much. "I wasn't expecting you to be so…tenacious, but it's okay. In the short time you've been here, I've only wanted to see you more. It feels right being with you again. I know I don't have the power to ask this, but I'm going to overstep my bounds a little." He watched her expectantly. "What do you say, Jade? Wanna give this crazy thing a shot?"

She thought a minute, considering what he'd said. "How about we start by spending some time together and see where it leads?" Jade wasn't sure if that was the answer he was looking for, but it was all she had to offer and he didn't seem put off by it. Jade could tell he was genuine, but her trust was something he was going to have to earn.

"That's fair." Spencer leaned forward and spoke to the pilot, but he must have switched channels because Jade couldn't hear him. She had come to New York with the sole intention of reclaiming her company and making sure she did *not* marry Spencer. She hadn't expected him to be as authentic as he was or try to help her as much as he did. She had gone into this alone and had unexpectedly gained an ally rather than a husband. If nothing else, they could definitely run the business together.

The plane was closing in on Alexander International Tower, preparing to land. *So much for our tour*. Jade had missed out on the last half of it. Once they had safely landed, they took off their headsets and jumped out of the aircraft and onto the roof. They sprinted to get out of range of the blades and watched the copter take off again.

"Don't worry," Spencer said. "We can try again another time, and actually sightsee."

Jade laughed, taking the band out of her already-mussed hair and putting it back up properly. She felt lighter, somehow, having gotten everything off her chest. Well, almost everything... Spencer had his phone out again and was tapping at the glass screen.

"Do you need to get back to work?" Jade asked.

"Not yet," he said. After a few more taps, he turned the phone off and called the elevator. "I'm just doing something I should have done a while back."

"What's that?"

"Proving myself. I'm blocking Stacy Washington from my life." He smirked, clearly satisfied with his decision. Jade wondered why he hadn't done it before, but knowing the way Stacy had wormed her way into his life, she could kind of understand it. When someone like that gained a lot of influence through unsavory means, it was easy for them to turn, ruin a reputation and not lose a wink of sleep over it. It was something she had read about in books and watched play out on television, and there were the few times she'd seen it acted out in business.

When they entered the penthouse, Jade's boxes had disappeared.

"They've been stored in the other guest bedroom for now," Spencer reassured her. "And feel free to unpack and put things where you'd like. This is your home now, too." *My home, too.* It still sounded bizarre to her ears, but she forced herself not to think about it too much.

"I have something for you," Jade said. "I went over our contracts and made some changes for you to look over."

"Lead the way," Spencer said. Jade started up the stairs and Spencer followed her to her room.

"You don't have to worry about it now," she said, handing him the brown envelope. "Whenever you get the chance will be fine..." He ignored her, already taking the pages out to look over them. After flipping through the documents, Spencer let out a chuckle.

"Very thorough, aren't you, Jade?" He slid the papers back into their envelope. "And a little demanding, hmm-m?"

Jade was about to protest, but he was clearly holding back a laugh, so instead she said, "You know, I was thinking that we should have dinner tonight." Jade folded her arms defensively and raised an eyebrow at him.

"Do you mean like a date?" Spencer smiled, leaning back against the wall to look at her.

"If that's what you want it to be."

He mirrored her, crossing his own arms. "It would be a great way to get to know each other better, to catch up. I know I stay busy all day, and starting tomorrow, you'll be working, too. I want to cook for you tonight, though."

"You cook?" Jade shouldn't have been surprised, but it was unexpected.

Spencer shrugged.

"I try." He checked his watch and let his head fall back with a sigh. "Right now, I need to be getting back. Will you be all right? Do you need anything?" Jade sat on the edge of her bed.

"I'll be fine," she said. "And I look forward to seeing what you can do with a frying pan."

"Frying pan?" Spencer scrunched up his nose in mock disgust. "What is that? A southern thing?"

"Yeah, it is," she shot back. "But it's okay... I wouldn't expect a Yankee to know anything about food."

"You wound me," he said, pressing a hand to his heart. With his other hand, he opened the door. "I'll be sure to teach you a thing or two about food when I get back. Prepare yourself, Jade Saunders, for the meal of a lifetime."

"I'll be sure to do that." Jade followed him out into the hall, desperately wishing he didn't have to go. Now that they'd talked outside a social setting, she found that she was enjoying his company. He was more like the old Spencer who she'd loved when the pressure had been off. There were still questions he needed to answer, though. As he waved to her from the first floor of 'their' home, Jade knew that even if everything fell apart, she would still want to be close to this new Spencer Alexander.

The elevator doors closed without a sound before Jade pulled out her phone. She scrolled through her contacts and edited his number so that the name now read 'Spencer'. She tucked the phone into her pocket and leaned her elbows on the half-wall, surprised to discover that she couldn't wait for him to get back.

Chapter Eight

July 8

Jade marveled at the new office that, if the plaque on the front door was correct, belonged to her now. The walls were glass, giving her views of the cubicles before her and a fantastic view from the window. Inky industrial carpet covered the floor and dark-mahogany furniture decorated the rest of the room. Jade sank into the cushioned swivel chair and looked over the shiny new desktop computer that still had plastic protecting the screen.

A small sticky note sat next to the keyboard, wishing her luck with her new office. It was signed by Spencer. Jade couldn't help the small smile that crept onto her face.

As it had turned out, Spencer was a wonderful cook. When Jade had expressed her enthusiasm over his amazing red lentil curry, he'd laughed and promised to make dinner for them more often. They'd eaten in the sitting room with the TV on but not being watched. Jade had come to learn about Spencer in unintended ways. She had observed him as he'd talked. He had a habit of messing with his hair, one that she was sure he didn't indulge in at the office. Small tics would appear if he was nervous, like biting his lip or stumbling over his words.

Spencer had shared stories of his college years — the many courses he'd taken and the friends he'd made and subsequently lost. There hadn't been many people in Spencer's life who he could trust and that made him extremely paranoid.

Jade had told him about her own life, how she had devoted herself entirely to work and how her father had wholeheartedly begun teaching her everything he knew about business. She'd shared vacations taken with her parents, day trips with Paige and Clint and her failed relationships that she could never quite keep up with. There had been an awkward pause as she'd contemplated furthering her statement. Should she have told him that he had been the only man she'd truly loved? That dregs of those feelings were still there — had always been, even though she'd not realized it — and were growing each day she was with him?

Jade couldn't help but outwardly cringe when she thought about how close she'd come to ruining a perfect evening. She still had feelings for Spencer. There were no doubts about it. But she was going to have to try to get over past joys and heartaches if she were to move forward with him. The more she mulled it over, the more she wondered what it was she really wanted.

Jade cleared any thoughts that weren't work-related from her mind and turned on her computer before setting her fingers on the keyboard. It was nice to be working again, to be back in her element. She had finally received some assignments from her father — and even a few from Carlton Alexander himself. *Like father, like son. Carl can't even take a vacation.* If things went the way their parents wanted, Jade would fit right in with this family.

The day passed by in a daze. Jade spent most of it at the computer, catching up on everything she had missed. Every hour or so, someone would pop their head through the door, briefly introduce themselves then ask a question. She was still new to the company policies but answered as best she could or referred them to someone else. Then it was back to the monitor. It was about six in the evening when she heard the faint tap on the glass.

"Heard you'd never left," Spencer said. Jade's attention immediately snapped to the door. "I thought you might be ready to pack up."

Jade nodded, caught off guard by Spencer's sudden appearance, and she began to close out of her work. Spencer strode casually across the small space, hands in his pockets and eyes trained on the setting sun outside. Jade watched him from the corner of her eye and couldn't help noticing the attractive profile he created.

Stop it! Now isn't the time. Jade shut down the computer and stood. She slid her phone into the pocket of her navy-blue blazer and cleared her throat to get Spencer's attention.

"I thought we would go out tonight," he said, turning and already on his way to the elevator. "I don't want to hole you up in the penthouse, after all."

"And it would be good publicity if we're seen together," Jade added as she joined him in the tiny enclosure. The doors slid closed and Spencer released a dry laugh.

"Believe it or not, this about more than business and marriage, Jade," he said. "If we're going to work together at all, it will take more than one night of not arguing or being mad at each other to fix it."

Jade remained silent through the entire taxi ride until they reached a place called *Sushi Ginza Onodera*. Jade had never been the biggest fan of raw fish, preferring her seafood to be deep fried, but if it meant finding peace between them, it would be worth it.

No matter what, Jade thought to herself, *I will get all of my answers tonight*. It was the only way she could move forward, the only way she could ever forgive Spencer, and she wanted to be able to do that. Spencer gave the man at the front his name and they were immediately led through the golden-hued restaurant to a bar that stretched along the back wall. The unmistakable scents of ginger and fresh fish hit Jade, but it wasn't nearly as bad as she had anticipated.

After they had placed their orders, Jade didn't waste any more time.

"Spencer, whose idea was the marriage?" she asked. Spencer took a sip of his water before answering.

"I already told you… It was planned by our parents. They remembered how close we used to be and thought it would be a brilliant idea to bring us back together." He turned to her, resting his elbow on the bar beside him.

"And did you agree?"

"Didn't you?"

Touché.

"What I meant was…did you tell them what had happened? Between us?" Jade began to fidget with a napkin, twisting the paper around her fingers.

"No." Spencer sighed. "I wanted to when this all happened, but I couldn't. I couldn't tell them what I'd done to you." Finally, Jade saw her opportunity.

"So, why did you…?" Jade's voice faltered. She cleared her throat, forcing the thick emotions down. "Why did you turn me down like that?" She could see it happening all over again.

It was the day after graduation and the Alexanders were visiting for the weekend. There was a movie out that Bryce wanted to see, so his parents took him out for the day. With Timothy and Angela at work, it left Jade and Spencer alone at the Saunders' house.

Jade walked out into the blazing Texas sun. Spencer was taking advantage of the pool and, in her mind, things couldn't have been more perfect. She called him over, threading her fingers together nervously as she tried to stammer out the right words. When she finished, when she told him that she loved him, Spencer Alexander laughed, placed his hands on his hips and refused to meet her eyes.

He turned wordlessly, looking back at the crystalline water. Jade didn't know what else to do, so she fled. She didn't look back as she ran to her room, the only safe place left for her. Tears streaked her face and soaked through her pillow all night, and she awoke the next morning to a headache and the news that Spencer and his family had left early with little explanation.

Now, seven years later, Jade was with Spencer again, and she would finally get the answers she so desperately sought.

"Jade, I don't know if you've noticed, but I'm a mess," he started. "When it comes to work, I'm there. I'm…good at public speaking and motivating my team. I can do whatever the job requires. But that day, when you came up to me and told me you loved me and I saw it in your eyes… I guess I got scared and didn't know what to do or say. I certainly didn't mean to react the way I did, but that was what came out."

"Cutting me out of your life wasn't the right way," Jade said, but much of the hostility was gone. In fact, almost all of it was gone. The scar that had been on her heart for nearly a decade was fading. This was all she had wanted — an explanation direct from Spencer. "You could have called or texted or…something."

"I know that now. And that's why I'm trying to fix it." He paused as their plates were set before them, but she wasn't interested in eating and it seemed that he felt the same. "Jade, I loved you, too, but I was a dumb kid who believed that, at the time, a relationship would have held you back or stifled you. And by the time I had gathered my thoughts and figured out what to say to you, we were gone." He held his hands out, searching for the right words. "I shouldn't have run away. I should have gotten in contact… I know better now. Jade, I cannot begin to express how sorry I am for what I did to you. I just want a second chance."

Jade picked up her chopsticks, poking at the small rose of ginger on her plate. It sounded so simple, like something that shouldn't have been bothering her all these years. It was all bad timing and a stupid boy who didn't know how to express himself. Now he wasn't that stupid boy anymore. Jade set her chopsticks back down and turned to face Spencer, extending a hand.

"It's good to see you again, Spence," she said. He looked from her face to her hand and back again.

"What are you doing?" he asked with a small laugh.

"A do-over." She grabbed his hand from where it rested on the bar and shook.

"As friends?"

"As best friends, like we used to be" — Jade shrugged before adding — "at least for now." That spark of hope she'd watch smolder in his eyes erupted into a flame and Spencer beamed. Sure, she didn't trust him completely yet. That sort of thing would take time. But Jade was willing to take a leap of faith — as she'd said, *'at least for now.'*

Chapter Nine

July 10

As Jade lay in bed, her alarm clock ready to go off in a few minutes, she looked back on the past couple of days and reveled in what had been happening. Each night, she and Spencer sat a little closer together. They passed light touches inadvertently, usually with her hand straying too close to his. The previous night, Spencer had walked Jade to her room and stood in front of her, brushing her dark hair back from her cheek. She had frozen, her breath caught in her throat as she prepared for what was about to happen.

Jade's alarm clock began to buzz that it was time for her to get up. *Nothing happened last night*, she reminded herself. He had simply told her goodnight before leaving for his own room. Jade sat up in frustration and knocked the clock onto the floor, successfully silencing it. When she had been on the plane to New York, she hadn't even wanted to see him again. Now she struggled to catch up with her rampant feelings. Being with Spencer felt right, like they had never been apart, like that day so long ago had never happened.

Jade climbed out of bed and started her morning. There were a couple of opened boxes in her room overflowing with clothes. She would have to figure that out soon. *One of many things I need to work out.* After a quick shower, she dressed in a black pantsuit and bright red satin blouse. She told herself that she liked that shirt, and it wasn't at all because Spencer had had told her it was his favorite color. With an application of light makeup, a few bobby pins holding her hair back and plain black heels, she started downstairs.

Spencer was waiting for her. Dressed in a navy suit and sky-blue tie today, he was a vision. His hair was styled back, and he had his hands in his pockets, something he had always done when standing but that Jade was starting to notice more and more. Spencer let out a low whistle upon seeing Jade, his eyes sparkling with an impish smile.

"Good morning," he said. "Got any plans for today?"

"Work, as you well know. Why?" She stopped a few feet away from him, the memory of the previous night making her reluctant to get too close.

"Well, in my experience, when a beautiful woman dresses up like that, she's going somewhere other than work." Spencer began taking steps to close the distance between them. "Got a hot date for lunch?"

"Well, that depends," she said. "What are *you* doing this afternoon?"

"Tempting…" he said with a grimace. "I'm afraid I'll be in meetings from eleven until three. I know a place, though. I could get you a reservation for around one or so."

"Oh. I was thinking like a café or diner. Nothing too fancy." Jade wasn't one for fine dining in the middle of the day. But Spencer was already on his phone — taking care of the arrangements, no doubt.

"You should try some of the best food the city has to offer. If you let me know before you head out, I'll have the car ready."

"Okay." Jade didn't want to fight him on this. "No limo this time, all right?"

"Agreed." The silence that followed was almost painful. Jade certainly didn't know what to say next, but Spencer wasn't making any sort of movement to leave. He simply stood there, watching her. Then the doors to the elevator opened and they boarded.

Jade wished he would say something, anything, even if it was about the night before. The doors opened again on an empty corridor lined with doors. This was obviously Spencer's stop, but he made no move to get out. Instead, he turned to her with a torn expression.

"We should probably get to our offices," Jade finally said. "I'm sure everyone's waiting."

"Yeah, they are." He shifted closer to her. Jade didn't move. Spencer wrapped his fingers delicately around her wrist, pulling her closer. "Jade, I..." His voice trailed off, as though he wasn't sure what to say. He was struggling and she watched the war behind his eyes. He wanted to kiss her and, if Jade were being honest with herself, she wanted it, too. The moment only lasted a second before Spencer backed away.

"I'm sorry," Spencer muttered. "This is all so confusing." Before Jade could argue, he was out of the elevator. "See you at dinner tonight?"

"Yeah, see you at dinner," Jade called after him as soon as she remembered how to form words. Spencer waved goodbye to her and left to start his day. Jade smoothed down her shirt and did her best to pretend nothing had happened. She would think about it later. For now, she had more pressing matters to deal with.

Jade reached her office and sat at her desk. She booted up her computer and pulled up her emails. Aside from the barrage of company emails, there was one from Clint.

It was an update, with the offer to bring her back to Dallas and away from Spencer, should the need arise. Jade laughed to herself. He also mentioned that he would be sending her a surprise package toward the end of the month, so Jade had something to look forward to.

After replying to Clint, Jade sent a quick text to Paige, urging her friend to fly up already. She missed her friends and hearing from them only amplified that. She didn't tell Paige about the almost-kiss, though. She still wasn't sure what it meant or where all of it was going, but it was something she wanted to hold on to for now.

Jade also didn't tell her about how much time she and Spencer had been spending together or that she was beginning to feel like this *was* a good thing. She knew how excitable her friend was and wanted to work out her own feelings before she announced them to Paige, which was like telling the world. For the time being, she let Paige know that things had greatly improved with Spencer.

By the time one o'clock rolled around, Jade had gotten very little work done but had analyzed the interactions between herself and Spencer in their entirety. It was clear that there was something between them. There always had been. And Spencer clearly wanted to move forward, not that Jade minded in the least. But he was going to have to make the first move. That much was certain.

Content with her findings for the day, Jade grabbed her wallet from her bag and shot Spencer a text to let him know she was going out. She wasn't expecting a reply, but she got one back almost immediately.

"Everything's ready," she read the screen aloud. The elevator lowered her through the building. Jade had no idea where she was going but was ready to see what Spencer had arranged. A black town car was waiting for her when she stepped outside. *Subtle.*

Jade watched as they wove through the streets of New York, passing both Rockefeller Center and Carnegie Hall. Up ahead, she could see Central Park. She asked the driver where they were going, but he shrugged, telling her that he had strict orders not to say anything. Jade pouted in the back seat. *It wasn't like I would have known any of the restaurants around here anyway.*

The car stopped and the driver opened the door for her. She stepped out in front of two large skyscrapers that were at least eighty stories high. The driver directed her to the one on the right, to floor thirty-five. She took another elevator but was not prepared for the room awaiting her.

It opened up to a beautiful, round lobby with a reception desk to her right and stairs to her left. Soft gold lights from above gave the room a lavish yet comfortable feel, as did the large sitting area beneath them. A man with a white shirt, black vest and gelled hair welcomed Jade.

"We've been expecting you," he said when she gave her name, gesturing past a glass swan centerpiece in the middle of the room. Beyond, she could hear the dull hum of people chatting, along with the clinking of utensils on plates. As she rounded the corner, she was greeted with a split-level room with floor-to-ceiling windows overlooking Central Park. The ceiling itself had an enormous light fixture that looked like silver branches creeping across the plaster.

Dividers separated booths along the walls and round tables covered the remaining floor space. There was another divider where private rooms were sectioned off. The atmosphere was modern, but the accents and green view gave it a natural touch. The restaurant was busy but quiet, and Jade liked that.

She was led to a table that faced the park, handed a menu that read *Asiate*, and assured that someone would be with her shortly. She thanked the host and looked over the menu. Her phone *pinged* in her pocket, and she checked a message sent from Kindall. Up until this point, Jade had been avoiding her. Sure, it was rude, but she didn't feel ready to handle planning a wedding. Now, she didn't think it was a bad idea to hear her out. As she typed out a reply, Jade felt a presence next to her.

"Oh, I'm not ready to order ye—" She stopped when she recognized the redhead staring down at her with large hazel eyes. Without invitation, Stacy plopped down in the seat across from Jade. She crossed her legs and didn't say a word.

Once again, she was dressed in something that looked like it had been taken straight from the runway. It was a sleeveless black dress with a gold fabric flourish the size of a basketball on one shoulder and an asymmetrical knee-length hemline. Knowing what her profession was, Jade could safely assume that this was something Stacy had designed herself.

"Are you ready to order, ma'am?" a waitress asked politely. Jade tore her eyes from the woman across from her.

"Yes," she said, scanning the menu quickly. "A burger, please, medium...and some sparkling water. Do you want anything, Stacy?" Stacy's icy stare focused on the waitress and she shook her head sharply. Jade thanked the employee and handed her the menu. She sent her text and slipped her phone back into her pocket.

"We need to talk," Stacy said, tossing her straight, shiny locks over her shoulder. Jade leaned back in her chair. Stacy mooning over Spencer was one thing, but this was going to a whole new level.

"What is it you want to talk about?" Jade asked, even though she already knew.

"I know what you did," Stacy said. "Everything was fine, then suddenly Spencer doesn't want to see me anymore. Suddenly, I'm blocked and can't contact him in any way. Now even his family is ghosting me. I know it's all because of you."

"I haven't told anyone to do anything," Jade said honestly. "Spencer is a grown man who makes his own decisions." Then, something occurred to her. There was no way Stacy was here by chance. "Wait! Did you follow me here?"

"Do you know where we are?" Stacy asked, ignoring the question and leaning toward Jade. "We are in the Mandarin Oriental. Do you know what that is?" Jade didn't respond. "It's where I wanted to have my wedding—where I can't have my wedding because of *you*."

"Get to the point." Jade was tired of her already. She had seen acts like this a million times and wouldn't be intimidated by it.

"The point," Stacy said sharply, placing both perfectly manicured hands on the table, "is that I want you to leave and never speak to Spencer Alexander or our family ever again."

Chapter Ten

"Excuse me?" Jade laughed. "Did you say *our* family?" Of all the things she could say... *How delusional is this person?* Stacy was not amused, her face becoming bright red in either embarrassment or anger. Jade didn't have time for this, but before she could speak, Stacy started in.

"You don't understand what I've gone through to get where I am," she said, her voice hushed. She didn't seem to want to cause a scene, but her emotions appeared barely held in check. "The things I've done to claw my way to the top... I came from nothing, from absolutely nothing, and I will not let you take this away from me."

"I am not trying to take anything away from you or anyone else."

Stacy scoffed, making Jade pause and exercise the patience she used so often at board meetings.

Jade tried another approach. "Look… I'm sorry that he won't speak to you, but that was his choice, not mine."

"Do you really think everyone doesn't know why you're here? *Everyone* knows about the contracts and the arranged marriage. They go along with it because it's the Alexanders, but at the end of the day, they all think it's disgusting — forcing a man from a relationship so he can marry a stranger." Stacy shook her head. Even though Jade didn't like what she was hearing, she wouldn't give this woman the satisfaction of knowing she'd gotten to her.

"I'm not a stranger," Jade said with a bored expression. "Spencer and I were friends years ago. We practically grew up together. Do you even love him?" When in a situation like this, Jade found it was best to turn the tables against the offender and use the element of surprise. Stacy blinked as though she didn't understand the question. "Do you love Spencer?" Jade repeated when she didn't answer.

"Of course I do," Stacy said, her voice pitched high enough to turn a few heads. Jade leaned forward, her arms folded on the table.

"I don't believe you," she whispered. "Sure, you 'clawed your way to the top', but you *used* people like Spencer, good people like the Alexanders, to do it. You wouldn't have done that if you loved him." Stacy was fuming, but Jade had made her point and was done with the juvenile nonsense. "If you'll excuse me, Miss Washington, I'm about to eat and, quite frankly, you're ruining my view *and* my appetite."

Stacy's lips quirked in a smug smile.

"I didn't want to have to do this, but since you're not cooperating, I guess I have no other choice." She reached into her black clutch and pulled out her phone, holding it up but not turning it on. "On this device are several incriminating photos of Spencer, taken during our night together. If you aren't gone by tomorrow, I'll leak them to every tabloid in America. He'll be ruined—and it will be because of you."

"You're bluffing," Jade said. A lump formed in her throat, but she maintained her poker face.

"Are you willing to take that chance?" Stacy slid the phone back in her purse. "Willing to gamble Spencer's reputation over your pride, Jade? You're, what, twenty-six? I'm only twenty-three and I've done more for myself, by myself, than you can imagine. Let's face it. You don't matter—not to him, at least. It'd be best if you run on back to Dixie, darlin'."

Stacy stood, leaving Jade feeling defeated. She was right. Jade wasn't willing to gamble with Spencer's life. She had about twenty-four hours to work something out, but the odds didn't look to be in her favor. Jade watched the woman sashay from the restaurant just as the waitress arrived with her meal.

Jade felt sick to her stomach. She hadn't been able to eat much and, on her way out, had received a call from Kindall. Jade tried apologizing for not taking her calls before, but Kindall told her not to worry about it. She understood the stress of the situation and had been expecting something like that. After making sure they were still on for the fourteenth, Jade hung up and practically ran to the town car that was still waiting for her.

The entire ride home was filled with her doubts as Jade tried to come up with a plan. She could back out of the deal entirely, which would cause problems for both families and her businesses. She could just *not* do anything, but that would ruin Spencer's business, leaving her guilty and returning to Saunders' Metalwork even more defeated. What if she told Spencer what had happened? She didn't think there was much he could do about it, but knowing was half the battle, right?

And now that she had been reminded of the appointment with Kindall in a few days, not to mention Paige's anticipated arrival on the same day, Jade began to feel overwhelmed. Stress usually helped her through things. Stress was her motivation. At that moment, though, like most people on the planet, stress was an ugly, looming monster threatening to swallow her whole. Once she was in the empty lobby of Alexander Tower, she could breathe again. Jade felt safe in those walls.

The elevator opened and Jade stepped in with two female employees she didn't know and pressed the button for her floor. The women cast sideways glances at her but said nothing. At the third floor, they got out, and Jade knew there would be gossip circulating the offices for the rest of the day. Alone at last, Jade leaned back against the cool wall and took a deep breath.

Her solitude was cut short when the elevator stopped at the tenth floor. The doors parted and who should be standing there but Spencer Alexander. He lit up when he saw her, his heart-melting smile washing over Jade and filling her with warmth in a way she didn't expect. He got in with her and directed the machine to floor eighty.

"Is everything all right?" Spencer asked. "You seem a bit tense. Did you not like the restaurant?"

Jade wished that was all that was wrong.

"The restaurant was fine," Jade said. "Everything was good." She was still at war with herself over whether she should tell him everything now or wait until she saw him later that evening. Jade decided to go for it. "Stacy was there. She followed me to *Asiate*." Spencer's eyes closed and he pinched the bridge of his nose with his thumb and forefinger.

"What in the actual hell?" he mumbled. "What did she want?"

"About what you'd expect. She wanted me to leave New York, to go 'back to Dixie'. She thinks everything is my fault and that you don't want to see her anymore because I told you not to." Jade was staring at the door, catching each floor button as it lit up in her peripheral vision. At that point, she couldn't hide the annoyance in her tone. "She also says that she has pictures of you and her...together. She threatened to release them to the media if I don't comply."

"Son of a *bitch*." Spencer slammed his fist against the wall. Jade jumped. She had not seen him this angry about anything since he'd lost a video game to Bryce when he was sixteen. "Well, I can guarantee you that there aren't any pictures," he said. Jade had had no idea that telling him would upset him like this. She should have saved it until after work. "If there were anything of the sort, she would have tried to blackmail me weeks ago. I've been trying to get away from her for a while and she hasn't taken the hint. I *knew* I should have done something about this before you got here."

"I believe you, but maybe it would be best if I left, at least for a few days," Jade said, "in case she does have something on you or tries anything." Jade could handle this if it were about her, but this was about Spencer. Spencer turned to her slowly, reaching behind him to the elevator panel to press the large red 'Stop' button. The elevator halted with a jerk and Jade wobbled slightly.

"You're not serious." Spencer's bitter demeanor quickly shifted to one of disbelief and hurt. "Jade, you've been in town less than a week. I know that's not much, but —"

"No, it's not like that," Jade rushed. "I can't have you or your reputation ruined because of me. At this point, I feel like I'm causing more problems than I'm fixing. It would be a way to buy you some time before Stacy…does whatever she's going to do. And we're still trying to figure out how we feel about each other and —"

"I don't give a damn what Stacy does," Spencer said, his deep, even voice filling the space in the elevator. He crossed the confined area, pressing her farther into the corner and keeping her there. One arm rested above her and the other was on his hip. "I can't be sure where this is going, either, Jade, but the two of us might really have something here. I know how *I* feel and I'm ready and willing to take that chance. Are you?"

"Isn't there somewhere you have to be?" Jade began to squirm. She couldn't think clearly in here, especially not with Spencer acting like this. She could feel the heat of his skin, his closeness making her hold her breath in anticipation. She should confide in Paige and get her opinion as an outside source. She could even talk to Clint about it. She needed to clear her head and —

Jade's mind went blank when Spencer leaned down and crashed their lips together. It was nothing like she had earlier imagined it would be. It was feverish and hungry. It was the certainty that Spencer had in them as a couple, certainty enough for the both of them. In a flash, the gap between them closed, as though this one kiss was a promise from Spencer that things had changed and he wanted it all. When she recovered from the initial shock, Jade surrendered, pressing into him with an equal longing, opening her mouth to allow him more access.

Jade wrapped her arm around Spencer's neck as he rested his hand against the small of her back. It had been years since she had been kissed, and she couldn't think of a single person she would rather have kiss her than Spencer. This was something she had fantasized about, and it was better than she could have ever dreamed. Jade sighed against him and, as their mouths moved together and she gave in to him completely, there was nothing else. Nothing but her and Spencer, and *damn* if it didn't feel amazing.

"I wanted to do that this morning," Spencer said, pulling back breathlessly.

Jade already missed the contact and desperately wanted to drag him back down to her. She fought to control herself.

"I was too afraid, though." He watched her, his oceanic eyes serious. "I'm not afraid anymore, Jade, and you shouldn't be either…not of anything."

"I've always been brave, Spencer. There's never been a time I've backed down, especially to someone like Stacy, and you know that. But this is different. This isn't about me. It's about you and your family. And if it means I have to give up whatever this is that we have for a few days, then so be it. It seems like a small price to pay to make sure your family doesn't get slandered." Sure, it would be hell for her, but better to do it now than after Stacy had done her damage.

"Why don't you try and have some faith in me, then?" Spencer ran his fingers through her hair, pulling her forward so that their foreheads rested together. "Believe me when I tell you that she doesn't have any leverage. She was trying to scare and manipulate you because that's what she does best. You leaving is what she wants. Don't let her win, Jade. Don't let her destroy us." He brushed her lips with his again then whispered, "Trust me, Jade." It was enough to pacify her apprehension, at least for a little while.

"I trust you," Jade said. Spencer smiled, a dimple forming in his right cheek that Jade hadn't noticed before. As much as she wanted to kiss him again, she restrained herself, gently moving him away from her as what had happened sank in. She glanced nervously at the security camera perched in the corner.

Spencer was still smiling as he pressed the red button again and the elevator gave a shudder before restarting. It was a good thing there were multiple elevators in this building, or he would have had some issues to sort out. She looked to the camera again.

"I'm sure the security guards will have quite the story to tell," Jade said, straightening her clothes and readjusting her hair.

"I wouldn't worry too much about that," Spencer chuckled. "That camera is broken."

"So what are we going to do?" Jade asked. She still wasn't clear on the plan of action concerning Stacy and, as long as Jade was sticking around, she would be involved. "Are we going to ignore her?"

Spencer laughed darkly.

"Oh, no. If Stacy thinks she can get away with something like this, she is dead wrong." There was a look in his eyes...one that made Jade glad she wasn't on the receiving end of it. "I'm going to make sure everyone in both my and her circle knows that she not only stalked and threatened you, but that she also tried to blackmail me. Hell, I might even take it up with the police."

Jade pressed her lips together. While that hadn't occurred to her, it wasn't the worst idea that Spencer could have come up with.

The elevator came to a stop and, since there was a small group ready to get in, Spencer gave Jade a short goodbye before getting out. When she finally reached her office, Jade collapsed on her chair and slouched down as far as she could. She had learned something today, something that made the Stacy incident worth it. Even with the past and the pain, Spencer was willing to fight for her.

Chapter Eleven

July 14

"Remember to breathe," Spencer said, his eyes glued to the tablet in his hands. Jade slowly paced across the living room, drawing patterns on the floor and sometimes circling the furniture. Her heels clicked against the tile in a steady rhythm that was somewhat calming for her, but she could tell was starting to grate on Spencer's nerves.

"I'm not panicking, Spence. I'm excited." Jade checked her phone again, but there were no messages. Spencer hummed but didn't look up. Since she had come downstairs, he hadn't so much as glanced her way, which was a little annoying. She didn't know what he was doing, but it was obviously important.

Spencer had taken the day off from work to help her—or at least that was what he'd said. Jade was sure he was doing something for AI on his device. She wrung her hands. It was a big day. Not only was her best friend coming to see her, but they were also meeting with Kindall to start preparing for the wedding. Jade wasn't sure whether or not she was ready for all this right now. But with the deadline looming over her and still no word on the contracts, she didn't have much of a choice.

To add to her stress, Jade had woken up to a string of texts from Stacy, calling her out for telling Spencer about their 'meeting' and threatening her further. Jade, in a groggy state, had rolled her eyes and sent screenshots of the messages to Spencer before slamming her phone back on the nightstand and thanking God that she had the day off. If Stacy persisted, that would be evidence to use against her.

Banishing all thoughts of Stacy, Jade focused on the good news of the day. Spencer had sent a limo to the airport to pick up Paige about thirty minutes before. It was supposed to bring her straight to the penthouse, but Paige had texted her saying they had to make a stop first. She hadn't specified why, and that was what worried Jade. There was no telling what her friend was up to.

It didn't occur to Jade until a little after Paige's text to let her friend in on what had been going on between herself and Spencer. Surprisingly, the pair had fallen back into an old routine—the past erased—and had found that they still had an undeniable chemistry. It felt natural to be with Spencer, and Jade tried her best to convey those emotions in a lengthy text to her best friend.

As Jade walked past Spencer for the umpteenth time, he tossed his tablet on the table next to him, snagged her around the waist and pulled her down into his lap, eliciting a yelp. He pinned her arms to her sides and leaned in close, their noses nearly touching.

"If you don't calm down, I'm going to lock you in your room and send Paige back to Texas," he warned. Jade scoffed and squirmed, but Spencer held her in place. "You're not going anywhere until you promise to stop walking around me like that. It's distracting."

"How is it distracting? You're looking at your tablet."

"There's a sexy woman in my house slinking back and forth in front of me and you think I'm going to stare at a screen the whole time? It's like you don't know me at all."

Jade laughed and tried to escape once again, but Spencer wasn't having it. He pulled her tight against him, leaning over to steal a long kiss. It was at that moment that the elevator dinged and announced a visitor. Since where they were seated facing said elevator, Jade saw Paige's jaw-drop reaction once the doors opened.

"Paige, you're here!" Jade leaped from Spencer's lap, straightening her black pencil skirt and emerald button-down. Thankfully, Spencer hadn't messed up her carefully placed chignon, but he had done plenty of damage to her composure. Jade took in Paige's dumbfounded expression. Judging by her friend's open mouth and wide eyes, Paige hadn't received her text message. "What took you so long?"

"I, uh, got a hotel room—and now I'm glad I did," Paige said, rushing over to hug Jade. She was dressed in true Paige fashion, wearing a lilac paisley skirt and a white peasant blouse. "What the hell has happened over the last week?" she whispered.

"Check your phone," Jade replied. "I sent you a thing. I thought you were going to be staying with us."

"Oh, no. You know how I need my space, and apparently so do you." She pulled out her phone and began scrolling, while Spencer stood up and straightened his tie. "Plus, this hotel is near a Panera Bread, and a vegan girl's gotta eat." Paige finished reading through the novel-length text, her smile widening with each sentence. When she was done, she put her phone away and looked at Spencer.

"Spence, it's been too long." Paige rounded the couch to get to him. Spencer had a hand out to shake, but she swatted it away and wrapped him in a hug. Spencer was clearly at a loss with the five-foot-tall girl hanging from his neck. He looked to Jade for help, but she watched him with an amused smirk.

"Hi," he said, peeling Paige off himself. She was so tiny against his six-four frame that he appeared afraid he would break her. "It's nice to see you haven't changed much."

Paige didn't respond, only turned back to Jade and began telling her every detail of the trip. Spencer shook his head and went back to his tablet. Paige told Jade about how the Alexanders had given her the same treatment, sending their private jet for her, and she even mentioned Katie. Jade had almost forgotten about cheery Katie.

"We should probably get going, ladies," Spencer said after she and Paige had chatted for a few minutes.

"Wait... Where are we going?" Paige asked, looking to Jade rather than Spencer for her answer.

"I hate to throw this at you as soon as you arrive, but we're planning the wedding today."

Paige brightened immediately, a small squeal rising from her throat. She grasped Jade's hands and began bouncing up and down.

"You want me to help you?" she asked. "Because I can totally help you. I have so many ideas already! Darn it… I don't think I brought my scrapbook with me. When can we leave?" Jade placed both hands on Paige's shoulders, stilling and silencing her long enough to get a few words in.

"Of course you're going to help." Jade had forgotten how easy it was to fire Paige up. Still, her friend's support was something she needed right now. Her insides were knotting themselves at the mere thought of this meeting.

Jade still wasn't sure about the wedding. Sure, she and Spencer were closer than ever, and she would even go as far to say they were dating — not out loud, though. In the days following Stacy's initial threat, both of them had kept an eye on the news, but there had never been any scandal announced. Spencer had been right when he'd said there was nothing to worry about. Stacy was full of empty threats. Since then, Jade had allowed herself to explore her feelings about Spencer, and everything had simply clicked.

Now, with Paige tugging Jade toward the elevator and Spencer right behind her, Jade felt something she hadn't in some time. It was like when she and Clint had been together, and they would go out for the day with Paige. It was a rare occasion when Jade was giddy and playful, overcoming the knots that still weighed her down. It was like old times, only with Spencer, and she liked that a little more than she would admit.

Kindall's office, if it could even be called that, was on the fifteenth floor. The entire floor was hers, with several glass-walled rooms that held decorations and fabrics and a large dining area for testing centerpieces, dinnerware and layouts. There was even a huge room for her DIY projects, of which there were many. Jade thought it was a beautiful workshop, even if it was presently being dedicated solely to her engagement party and wedding.

When they entered, it was easy to spot Kindall. She was standing in the middle of the dining area with a clipboard, directing her employees on how many chairs should be at each table and what color the plates should be. She wore a teal shirt with silver stitching tucked into high-waisted black slacks and low heels. Jade caught her eye and she smiled, waving the small group over.

"I'm so glad you're here," she said. She introduced herself to Paige without a prompt, complementing the shade of purple she wore. Paige leaned over to Jade.

"I like her," she whispered.

"We have a lot to go over, so I suggest we get started." Kindall was practically shaking with anticipation. Jade could tell that she was someone who loved her job.

"Show us what you've got," Spencer said. Kindall didn't waste any more time and led them to one of the rooms that was covered with swatches, photographs and place settings. Fabric of every color of the rainbow was in there, draped neatly over a set of chairs, and there was a shelf along the wall that held dozens of binders, each marked with an event and a year. Kindall pulled two of them out and set them on the table in the middle of the room, gesturing for them all to sit.

"I'm sorry to say this, but you don't have much say in your engagement party. We had to go ahead and plan it since it'll be held in about three weeks. But, don't worry… We have some options for you to choose from." She went through the list on her clipboard, describing a simple cocktail theme, a black-tie casino theme and a masquerade ball. Jade didn't even have to think about it.

"I've always wanted to go to a ball," Jade said, looking to Spencer for his opinion.

Spencer shrugged.

"Sounds good to me," he said. "You can send out the invitations later today." Jade smiled at Paige, remembering when they had been little and would dress up as princesses. Wedding or not, Jade would enjoy at least one party in Manhattan while she was there. After choosing colors and approving the invitations, Kindall pulled out another binder, this one labeled 'Alexander Wedding 1'. There were sticky notes and bookmarks erupting from the stuffed notebook.

"You have a little more say over the wedding, but both the Saunders and Alexanders have given me ideas, since we're pressed for time. I think I've managed to combine them all into something everyone will like." She went through, describing a fall forest-themed wedding. Cuttings of burgundy velvet and orange tulle were laid before Jade. An assistant brought in bouquets of live roses and dahlias. Dress designs were snuck over to her, far from Spencer's curious gaze. It all looked so magnificent.

"I really don't know what to say." Jade looked over the materials spread out before her. It was planned to be the perfect fairytale wedding, the kind any woman would dream of, but her pulse was racing at the mere mention of it. At this point, Jade was ready to leave and spend some time with Paige. "I love the theme, and the colors are perfect. I think we'll go with what we have here, if that's all right."

"That's perfect. It would look great in Central Park with the turning leaves," Kindall suggested. That was where Jade was able to give some input. If this was happening, it would not be outside. She had seen pictures of her parent's beach wedding and, though they loved the memories and laughed about them now, it had been a disaster.

"I would prefer an indoor wedding," she said. Kindall began scribbling notes down. "And I don't want a lot of people, either. Family and close friends only."

"An exclusive wedding. Love it." Kindall turned to the back of the folder and rattled off a list of venues. Kindall's first pick was the Mandarin Oriental, which Jade immediately shot down with a knowing glance to Spencer. She also saw images of 620 Loft and Garden and the Brooklyn Botanical Gardens, but Jade was adamant that the wedding would be indoors.

After going through a few websites and making some calls, they had a ceremony and reception area booked at Weylin and would be touring it later the next month. Kindall kept apologizing for the rush of things, but with only a few weeks left to plan an elite New York wedding, it had to be done this way. Jade understood and was mainly relieved that everything was already taken care of. It was one less thing for her to worry about.

"Now that most of that's out of the way," Kindall said, standing up. "I think it's time we divide and conquer. Jade, I understand you're going to have Paige as your maid of honor, correct? No other bridesmaids?"

"That's right." She and Spencer had talked about it briefly and agreed that it would be just them with Paige and Bryce by their sides. Jade found that she was much more comfortable discussing these things with him. It didn't feel as serious, like it had when they were kids playing pretend again without all the weight of responsibility. Kindall nodded and dug a business card from the binder.

"Your last mission is to go to this shop and tell them it's for the Alexander wedding. They'll accommodate you with whatever you need. You're not expected to make a decision today, but please do so as quickly as possible." She shooed the girls from her office, claiming that she and Spencer had their own list to get started on.

"Wait! What kind of things are on your list?" Paige demanded, obviously never wanting to be left out of anything. Kindall cut her eyes to Jade, who was a few feet away, and leaned in to whisper something to Paige. The small woman began to cackle maniacally, as Kindall raised her voice enough for Jade to hear her make her friend swear not to say anything.

"No promises," Paige sang.

"What is it? What are they planning?" Jade couldn't help asking.

"Nah, I think I'll save it." Paige tapped her fingertips together like some supervillain who had come up with a dastardly scheme. Jade rolled her eyes and told herself that she didn't care anyway. She wasn't going through with this wedding.

Am I?

They boarded the elevator and hit the button for the ground level, where Jade knew there would be a car waiting for them. There always was. She flipped the card over in her hands, finally reading where they were headed. She groaned as the embossed gold letters simply read *Timeless Bridal Boutique.*

Chapter Twelve

Of course Kindall's sending us to a bridal boutique...

The second Jade and Paige stepped into the shop, a small bell jingled and they were met with the scents of bergamot and honey. It was an old-fashioned store with a tearoom theme, gold-leaf details, delicate lace, pink porcelain decorations and antique light fixtures. There was a small reception area off to the side with a curtained entrance to the back, but no one was there.

"This is not at all what I was expecting," Jade said, taking in the lounge.

"What *were* you expecting?" Paige asked. She bounced over to the reception desk and tapped the small bell, sending another ring throughout the store.

"Just a minute!" someone called from the back.

"With the way this wedding is going so far, maybe something a touch more modern?" Jade shrugged. She picked up a hand-stitched doily, wondering why Kindall would have sent her to this place. "I don't think we'll find anything that's particularly 'me' here."

The floral-patterned curtains that hung behind the reception area parted, and out stepped a tall, elderly woman. Her hair was up in a strict bun and she wore a pastel pink fifties-style dress and glasses. She smiled warmly, circling the desk to clasp Jade's hand.

"You must be Jade. Kindall said you'd show up today," she said. "My name is Francine and I'll be assisting you." She pulled Jade along to the back, motioning for Paige to follow. "Don't you worry about a thing. We may look old-fashioned, but we've had designs on the Paris runways." The back room looked like something from a dream, though certainly not Jade's. White ball gowns lined the walls, rolls of tulle and fabric were spread over tables and in the very back was a lit platform surrounded by mirrors. Jade swallowed a lump that had formed in her throat.

"This is my granddaughter, Candace," Francine said. A much younger girl, who was pinning muslin to a dress form, grunted out a greeting. She was dressed similarly to Francine and barely acknowledged them, too focused on her work. Francine headed farther back, where she pulled out a rack with several wedding dresses, as well as some burgundy bridesmaids' options. Jade could tell that this was a small, family-owned business and commended Kindall for not using a large designer shop.

"We set aside some pieces for you to look over. Feel free to try on any of them, and I'll be right here if you need anything." Francine was beaming. "You're going to make the prettiest bride, dear." Jade swallowed hard and stepped up to the rack, pulling aside hangers with a shaky hand to get a better look at the gowns. Paige was by her side, looking over the red dresses.

This was becoming too real for her. Things weren't supposed to go this far. Jade had never been one of those girls who fantasized about her wedding in expansive detail, so she had no clue what kind of dress she wanted. Should she pick the enormous ball gown with pearl detail? What about the evening gown with gold embroidery along the side? *Where is Kindall and her epic decision-making?* Jade snatched the first dress off the rack without looking and Francine directed her to a changing room.

"I'll help her out. Thanks," Paige said, following Jade into the room and shutting the door. "What is going on? Are you okay?" Jade had collapsed onto a tufted bench, gasping in breaths, the ball gown splayed over her lap.

"I'll be fine," she said. "Give me some time." Paige knelt beside her. In all their years of friendship, she had been the dependable one and usually looked after Paige. Now, it seemed it was her friend's turn to be there for her.

"Hey, listen to me." Paige wrapped an arm around Jade's shoulders. "I'm right here, okay? I know this is terrifying, but you can handle it. You're Jade-freaking-Saunders!" Jade laughed at that, leaning into Paige, who went on. "Now, you get up and you put that fancy dress on, even though you would never wear something like it in your life."

"I wouldn't, would I?" She held up the dress that she had picked and sighed. The body and sleeves of the gown were beaded with pearls. She didn't even like pearls that much. "I'm scared, I guess."

"Are you scared of falling in love with Spencer, or is it something else?" Paige asked, though she probably already knew the answer. "I saw you two earlier, and you were never like that, not even with Clint. You looked like you used to when the Alexanders would come down for the summer. You looked…happy."

"There's something about him," Jade said. "Something that I like, that I always have… I admire his work ethic." At this, Paige scrunched up her face. "No, that's stupid. Oh, Paige, it's more than that. When we're alone, he's so easy to talk to, and he's been wonderful to me from day one, even though I acted like an ass. Once we cleared the air, things just…worked. We didn't even have to try. He's great, and yes, I still have feelings for him, but is that enough to build a marriage on? I don't even think I want to get married yet!"

"That's a good question, love." Paige gave Jade a small squeeze. Jade knew that she wanted to help more than anything. "I don't think it would be healthy if you didn't have doubts. For now, since it's right in front of us, let's see what we can do about this." She fluffed the tulle skirt. "Then we'll see about everything else. Take it one step at a time." Jade nodded her agreement.

Paige helped her into the dress, but she knew immediately that she didn't like it. She gave it a fair chance, though, stepping up onto the platform and doing the obligatory twirl, but it wasn't her. Jade tried two more, and while the fit was perfect, Jade couldn't see herself walking down the aisle in any of them. Francine looked over the selection on the rack then asked Jade a series of questions. After making some notes, Francine told her not to worry and promised that on her next visit she would have the perfect gown ready for Jade to try on.

On the ride back to AI, Jade and Paige caught up. Jade asked how Paige's family was and how her career was doing. Though Paige's parents worked within her father's company, Paige owned a small art supply store in Dallas. Paige's art had been featured in galleries all over America. Jade listened as Paige babbled about trying to show in Europe and Japan, finding comfort in her voice.

When they reached AI, Jade said goodbye to Paige. She was staying at the Park Terrace Hotel, which was only a few blocks away, and wanted to catch some sleep. As much as Jade wanted her to stick around, she would be able to survive the rest of the day.

"I was so excited that I was up all night," Paige explained with a yawn. After Paige's promise to call her later, Jade went into AI, thinking of how good her own bed would feel right about now. She was still in a daze when she entered the penthouse and was caught off guard when she saw Spencer in the kitchen.

"You're back early," he said. He had changed out of his suit and was now in gray sweatpants that sat low on his hips and a black T-shirt, which, in Jade's opinion, was a little too tightly stretched across his chest.

"So are you," she said, dropping her wallet on the counter and sitting across from him. He was preparing grilled-cheese sandwiches and, without having to ask, took out a couple more slices of bread for hers. "Don't you have work you should get back to?"

"I already told you that I took the day off. And, while I was at it, I decided we should both take the rest of the week off," he said, not looking up from where he was smearing butter over the bread.

"Because your dad's coming back tomorrow?" Jade asked.

"It helps. He can handle things for a bit while I'm not there." He looked up at her. "Also, Paige texted me.

She has always been an amazing friend and is very protective over you."

"When did you give Paige your number?"

"Kindall made a group text with the four of us. She said it was for, and I quote, *'wedding emergencies'*. You probably have some texts to catch up on." Jade crossed her arms on the surface before her and buried her face. "Look... I wanted to do this, if that's what you're wondering. Paige just gave me the nudge."

Jade's face heated up.

"So, you're taking an entire week off from work to spend time with me?"

"Yep." Spencer moved over to the stove, tossing the first sandwich on the griddle. "I've already planned some activities, too. We're going to go on that tour, spend a day on the water, watch a Broadway show... You know, I've lived here most of my life and I've never been to one." He turned his head to look at her. "It'll be fun."

Jade mustered up a smile for him. The conversation with Paige was still fresh in her mind, but she didn't want to bring that up again—not with Spencer. When his attention was turned back to their lunch, Jade's smile faded. Maybe this upcoming week with him would be what she needed to make a decision.

As soon as they had eaten, Jade excused herself and headed upstairs. She needed a few more minutes to herself. Deciding to be productive, she turned in to the spare bedroom that was stuffed with her boxes. She had the two boxes of clothes in her room, but there were another three there. Then there were her boxes filled with family photos, decorations and kitchen appliances. The kitchen stuff was what was taking up the most space, and Jade decided that most of it could be donated. She could always buy new stuff when she returned to Dallas, right? *If I return to Dallas...*

Jade swallowed hard and got to work. She opened boxes in silence, sorting through her belongings on autopilot. She didn't know how long she had been at it, but she'd gone through almost everything and had a large donation pile. That was when Spencer walked in.

"Is there anything I can do to help?" he asked quietly from the doorway. Jade straightened, tossing a flattened cardboard box onto the bed and turning to him.

"I think I've got this part covered," she said. Spencer stepped in and picked up a framed photo from the floor. It was one of her when she had been eight, with her parents on either side. He chuckled and held it out to her.

"I'm serious," he said. "We should put some of this stuff up to make it a little homier around here. This apartment needs redecorating."

"Well, what I need is somewhere to put all these clothes." She pointed to the three boxes that had been set aside, not even mentioning the two in her own room. Between events with her parents and business meetings, Jade had acquired quite the wardrobe.

"I think I know a place." Spencer picked up two of the boxes effortlessly, the muscles in his arms and back flexing beneath the thin material of his shirt. *Stop that*, she chided herself before her imagination went too far. *This is not helping your dilemma.* All the pros and cons and lists she had made in her head disappeared as quickly as if they'd never been there. Jade picked up the other box and followed Spencer into the hallway.

He surprised her by opening the door to his room. Jade paused before going in after him. Spencer's bedroom wasn't anything special. She didn't know what it was she'd been expecting, but a tidy bedroom that was like the other bedrooms in the apartment hadn't been it. It wasn't like her apartment, with memories and special knickknacks scattered along walls and shelves. There was nothing on his walls, only towering windows with a view like hers.

"Over here," he said, swinging open two doors that were definitely not in the other rooms. Inside was one of the biggest closets Jade had ever seen. A little less than half was covered with suits, ties, formal wear and dress shoes. The rest was empty. Had he been expecting her to move in here or did he simply not own enough to fill the space? She preferred not to think about it too much.

"You're welcome to come in here anytime," Spencer said. When he saw how Jade was glancing around, he clarified, "I know it's pretty bare, but I just moved in a week before you got here, so I haven't had time to do anything with the place yet. Most of my stuff is still packed away at my parents' house."

She looked at him and smiled.

"You have this habit of knowing exactly what I'm thinking," she said. "You always have. Am I that easy to read?"

"Can I tell you a secret?" Spencer leaned in and whispered, "I'm actually bad at reading people." He straightened and began moving the boxes into the closet. "It's part of the reason I'm so terrible with personal relationships. But I don't know... With you, it has always been different. We've always had a connection." He stopped and leaned back against one of the shelves, laughing. "I'm sorry. That sounded stupid."

"No, it didn't," Jade said. Together, she and Spencer filled the other side of the closet with her clothes then worked through the rest of the piles. Pictures and baubles found their way across the apartment. Spencer called for someone to come collect all the donated items and recycling, and, when Jade looked around the apartment again, there were pieces of her life scattered around. A warmth spread through her. Spencer's apartment felt a little more like home now.

Her gaze landed on a particular frame that sat in the center of the mantle. Jade didn't remember packing it. She didn't even remember owning it. Her mother must have snuck it from their home and into her boxes. Twelve-year-old Spencer and ten-year-old Jade sat on a hospital bed. Spencer had a fresh bandage over his left eyebrow and was giving a goofy smile and thumbs-up to the camera. Jade had her arms slung around his neck, eyes red from crying, but was laughing at whatever he had said before the picture had been snapped.

Chapter Thirteen

July 19

The midday sun bore down on Jade, Spencer, Paige and Bryce as they boarded the Alexanders' yacht, *The Absolution*, from the swim platform.

Spencer and Bryce were shoving each other playfully as they filed through a narrow, covered hall, arguing about who would get to steer. Paige and Jade were right behind them, caught up in their own conversation. Gulls called from the dock, and the warm, salty sea air was heavy around them. A soft breeze tugged at Jade's clothes. She couldn't recall the last time she'd felt like this.

The past few days had been blissful. Jade and Spencer had seen a Broadway show and gone on a fantastic helicopter ride over Manhattan again—this time, without any distractions, Spencer had been able to point out all the landmarks that she'd missed the last time. Paige had been more than happy to be the third wheel on many of their outings, but gave them their space now and then. When they weren't out on some new adventure, they were holed up in the penthouse with takeout and bad reality shows to keep them company. It was like she was sixteen again, goofing around with Spencer.

"You guys get settled," Spencer said as he headed inside with Bryce. "We'll cast off." Jade didn't miss the wink Bryce threw at Paige. She had to admit that Paige was different today. She was showing off the body that she always hid under baggy clothes, sporting a rainbow-striped string bikini, and her blonde hair contrasted well against her tanned skin. All in all, she looked stunning.

Jade was wearing a royal blue one-piece with cutouts on the sides and lacing along the back. She had thrown a black sundress over it and wouldn't be taking it off until they went swimming. Her hair was pulled back into a loose fishtail braid that would also come down once she was in the water.

The lounge area that opened up from the hall was sheltered, with couches, chairs and pillows scattered around a small table. Set against the wall was a full bar, a state-of-the-art grill and a TV that dropped from the ceiling. Jade didn't want to go inside yet, especially after spending so much time indoors — not that her time had been unenjoyable.

Jade smiled to herself, remembering how she had woken up that morning next to Spencer. They had both fallen asleep in the sitting room on a small cot that Spencer had made from several comforters and pillows. Jade couldn't deny that she liked waking up next to him. When he slept, his breaths were deep and even, his lips slightly parted and his face peaceful. She closed her eyes, willing the thoughts into the back of her mind before turning to Paige.

"What was that?" Jade asked, referring to Bryce's flirtations. Paige lay across a couch, adjusting her sunglasses and shrugging innocently. "Come on, Paige. He's only eighteen."

"What's seven years' difference? He's cute!" Paige joked. "Don't worry... You know I'm not going to do anything. He's a flirt, anyway."

Jade nodded. One day, that would get Bryce in trouble. She sat down across from Paige, sheltered from the blazing sun. Sweat was beginning to cling to Jade's skin, and she could feel her skin burning already despite the sunscreen she'd applied on the way over.

The boat tilted slightly, taking them out to sea. What was once a breeze turned into a full gust, and Jade could imagine the boys at the bridge, seeing how fast they could go before she and Paige started yelling at them. Jade gripped the arm rests and closed her eyes, a refreshing mist of sea water hitting her every so often. Paige appeared to be sleeping.

When they were far out to sea, the boat slowed to a cruise then stopped altogether. Bryce was the first one down.

"Having a good time, ladies?" he asked. Paige let out an overexaggerated snore from her seat, to which Jade cackled. "I see how it is," Bryce said, pretending to be hurt.

"Where's Spencer?" Jade asked, standing. Bryce was lowering the anchor with a button. Far behind him, Jade could see the jagged teeth of the Manhattan skyline.

"Right here." Spencer's deep voice was directly behind Jade, causing goosebumps to prickle across her skin. She simultaneously loved, hated and didn't understand how he had that kind of effect on her. She turned to Spencer, who was sporting gray board shorts and a white shirt, his sunglasses propped on top of the dark mess on his head that he called hair. He was smiling down at her, his height much more pronounced now that Jade wasn't wearing heels.

"Hey, have you seen this?" Bryce had his phone out, and Jade pouted at Spencer.

"How come he gets to bring his phone and I don't?"

"Bryce isn't the one in serious need of a vacation," Spencer shot back.

"Yeah, Jade. I just got back from mine." Though his tone was playful, he hadn't looked up from his screen, his lips set in a thin line. Whatever he was looking at couldn't be good. Spencer stood behind his brother, and his face immediately fell when he saw what it was. Bryce slowly turned the phone to Jade.

The screen was opened to one of Stacy's social media pages. It showed her in a salon, her bright red tresses now dyed an inky black. *Such a shame,* Jade thought. *Her hair might have been her best feature. She does pull the dark hair off, though.* One look at Spencer and she knew that he thought differently.

"She's probably trying out a new look." Jade said. She wasn't sure why she was defending this woman, but she was sure that it was, in part, due to not wanting to admit what was probably really going on. She also wouldn't allow Stacy's childish actions to ruin a perfect day with her friends.

"I think we all know that's not the case," Spencer said darkly. He took Bryce's phone and tossed it onto one of the chairs. "I can't believe her. And she knows there's nothing we can do about it. She's taunting us."

"Hey, let's not touch Bryce's phone. How does that sound?" Bryce mumbled. Spencer laughed, already back to his old self with no trace of anger. The eldest Alexander brother tugged at the hem of his shirt, pulling it over his head. Jade drank in his muscular chest, which had a light dusting of brown hair. His trunks were hanging low on his narrow hips, with a strip of dark hair trailing from his navel and disappearing below his waistband. The last time she had seen him at their pool, he had been starting to develop muscles, still lean and awkward from his teenage years. This was a change she liked.

Paige cleared her throat behind Jade. She looked to see her friend, sunglasses lowered on her nose, wiggling her eyebrows at her. Jade rolled her eyes at Paige's immaturity but could feel her body heating in all sorts of ways. She didn't mean to stare, but her gaze kept drifting back to Spencer. She could always blame her sweating on the sun, right?

"Shall we?" Paige suggested, standing up from the couch and giving Jade a poke in her ribs before stepping up to the railing. She tossed her sunglasses onto the couch next to Spencer's discarded pair, stretching her arms to warm up.

"Why not?" Jade released the knot from the back of her dress and yanked it off, then did the same with the band in her hair, shaking out her tresses. She approached the railing, standing next to Paige, then glanced over her shoulder and caught the way Spencer was watching.

Bryce was the first one in the water, cannonballing enough to spray those still on board. Paige went in after, diving so gracefully that she barely made a ripple. Spencer and Jade were the last ones in the water. The

Atlantic was cool and pleasant. Jade stayed submerged for a few seconds, relief washing over her scorching flesh.

When she resurfaced, Jade was caught in the middle of a war that had been started by Paige and Bryce. She and Spencer joined in, boys versus girls with no rules. Splashing, swimming beneath an opponent to drag them under from behind... It was mayhem and no one was keeping score. Jade couldn't think of when she'd last had this much fun with her friends. A moment of guilt hit her. She had never had this much fun with Clint.

As she'd been forced to do lately, Jade buried the thought. She refused to feel bad now. Suddenly, Paige dropped beneath the surface with a short scream. Bryce surfaced nearby, swimming away as fast as his arms could carry him. *Smart boy*, Jade thought. Paige had been on the swim team in high school and was still in practice. As she watched her friends swim farther and farther away, she felt the water ripple around her. She was about to turn to defend herself when a hand brushed at the wet tendrils of hair clinging to her neck.

"Having a nice time?" Spencer asked, his voice dripping with something she'd never heard from him. Jade's heart bruised her chest and she found that she couldn't form words. Beneath the water, Spencer wrapped an arm around her waist, pulling her back against him as he played with one of the side holes on her bathing suit with his thumb. He pressed his lips to her shoulder, dragging them up along her neck, where he began to whisper.

"I wonder what possessed you to wear such a thing." Spencer pressed his fingertips into Jade's skin, but she could tell he was holding back. "If you were trying to get my attention, you already had it." Still at a loss for words, Jade turned to face him, staring up into his eyes.

"What has gotten into you?" she asked, trying hard to sound light but failing as her words wavered. Spencer cracked his half-smile.

"I'm not sure," he said, his sultry tone coaxing her under his spell. "There's just something about you, something about today. Maybe it's been a long time coming and now it feels like we're ready." With that, he bent down and kissed her.

He hadn't kissed her like that since the elevator, and Jade was quickly reminded of what that had done to her. She pushed up into his kiss as Spencer held her close to him. God, she used to want this more than anything, and the reality was far better than anything she could have imagined. His expert mouth moved with hers, not dominating but still a touch demanding. A nearby splashing startled Jade, and she broke the kiss to see Paige and Bryce swimming back their way.

Dizzy and with her breathing labored, Jade suggested they climb back onto *The Absolution* to rest and grab a bite. Whatever magic had been holding them together had begun to wash away, but Jade could still feel it inside. She reluctantly pulled away from Spencer and followed Paige up the ladder. The air was cool against her soaked skin, and she blamed the goosebumps on that. When they were all topside, Bryce fired up the grill and the group followed him inside to the full kitchen and dining room. There was another lounge inside, similar to the one they'd just left, only with air conditioning.

"Fancy," Paige commented. She plopped down at the dining table and rested her chin on the heel of her hand. Bryce unloaded the fridge. Jade felt a hand wrap around her waist and tug slightly. Spencer jerked his head to the side, signaling for her to come with him. A little thrill ran through her, causing her to smile nervously.

"I wanted to show you the rest of the boat, if you're interested," he said. The right side of his mouth was quirked in that smile that could make Jade agree to anything. Spencer led her up a set of stairs to a little room that sat atop the boat. Outside the window was a sky lounge. *This yacht is definitely meant for parties that involve more than four people.*

"This is the helm station," Spencer said, pointing to four screens and a panel below them, which housed several knobs and switches. Jade looked the setup over but didn't dare touch anything.

"Looks complicated," she said. Every nerve in her body was aware that she and Spencer were alone together in the little room, but she tried to ignore the feelings that came along with that. "A full kitchen, dining room and three separate hangouts... What else is on this thing?"

"Well, there are also four bedrooms and five bathrooms on board." He leaned in close and said, "We sailors call a bathroom 'the head'."

"So, you're a sailor now, too?" Jade laughed. Spencer's light attitude helped relieve some of the tension, but she caught his blue gaze roaming her barely clad body. Jade hugged herself, feeling exposed and more than a little chilly.

"May I?" Spencer offered her his hand. She took it and followed him back down the stairs. Instead of taking a right to the kitchen, where Bryce and Paige could be heard deep in conversation, Spencer turned left into a large master suite. There were narrow windows set horizontally around the room, through which Jade could only see ocean and sky. The bed was neatly made and took up a large portion of the room. Spencer shut the door behind him.

She turned to face him, her chest heaving with each breath, her nerve endings like lit matches under her skin. Spencer was crossing the room slowly, seeming to enjoy the effect he was having on her. Lightheaded and more than a little intoxicated by Spencer, Jade took in his form. The layer of salt water that clung to his muscles shone in the light and Jade longed to reach out and run her hands down his chest. Only then did she realize that she was worrying her bottom lip between her teeth.

"Spen—" Before she could get his name completely out, Spencer had pressed his soft lips to hers, sending that delicious heat through her veins. He dropped his hand to the small of her back and cupped her face gently with the other. Spencer was slow with his ministrations, taking all the time in the world before swiping his tongue across her lips, deepening the kiss. He moved her backward at the same pace until the backs of her knees hit the bed and she dropped to the mattress.

As Spencer hovered over her, Jade acted on instinct, wrapping a leg around him. She needed him to be closer, to be a part of her. Spencer seemed all too happy to comply, grinding his hips against hers with a low groan. Jade felt the hardness straining beneath his swim trunks and gasped.

With their kiss broken, Jade saw how flushed Spencer's cheeks were, how his lips were swollen and his already-dark eyes had turned nearly black. She only got a second to take all of that in as he covered her with his body and continued what he had started. He trailed his lips down her jaw, to her neck and collarbone. She pushed into the touch, high on the sensations it sent throughout her.

"Spencer," Jade moaned. He froze and raised up to look at her. All those wonderful feelings from the day were replaced with embarrassment. She hadn't meant to do that, and Spencer's face was unreadable. All the last week had been spent reconnecting, and now she might have ruined it in one fell swoop.

"Jade." He said her name reverently, smoothing away any fears she might have had. He kissed her softly, allowing his fingers to trace down the side of her still-damp bathing suit, making contact with her feverish skin at the cutouts. Jade, in turn, threaded her hands in his hair. New feelings were taking over, things she didn't know how to handle. She began to pull away.

"Is everything okay?" he asked.

"It's fine. I... I don't want to ruin this." She didn't want to move away from him, though. "Things are happening kind of fast and there are still...doubts. I mean...with the wedding being pushed —"

"It's okay," he said. "I would never ask for more than you're willing to give, Jade." He smiled at her, and it was clear that he was telling the truth. "That being said, there is no way you could ruin anything happening here. But I'll take things a little slower if that's what you want." This time, she was the one to push up and demand a kiss, to which Spencer complied. Then a knock echoed from the door.

"Um, guys? Food's ready." Bryce's voice floated in. He sounded tentative, and Jade knew he and Paige had likely played 'rock, paper, scissors' to see who would come to drag them away from whatever they were doing. Spencer held a finger to his lips with an evil gleam in his eye. Jade covered her own mouth to stifle a giggle.

"Give us, like, ten minutes," he called back to his undoubtedly mortified brother. Jade smacked him arm, but Spencer laughed and leaned down to kiss her again.

Chapter Fourteen

July 26

A week later, Jade stood in front of *Timeless Bridal Boutique* with Paige. She wasn't sure why they were outside in this simmering heat instead of inside the air-conditioned building, but she expected it to be worthwhile. She pulled her hair up, giving the nape of her neck a short break from suffocation. Jade had changed as soon as she'd gotten off work and now wore a soft blue tea dress. It had been a gift from Spencer, and she was glad she'd changed, because the light material was beginning to cling to her. She couldn't imagine still being in her pantsuit. Jade shifted her weight, her tan wedge sandals becoming very uncomfortable on the concrete.

"Can't we wait inside?" Jade asked. She hated to whine, but she couldn't remember the last time she'd sweat this much.

"No, we have to be waiting right here." Paige had not allowed Jade to go inside, even though they could both see Kindall through the window. Paige was probably even hotter than Jade, with a long, sleeveless denim dress and a colorful scarf tied around her waist. She'd obviously tried her best to pull her hair back and the small bun she'd managed to create bounced as she moved with excitement. There was a sharp slam behind Jade and Paige as Kindall stomped out of the store and joined them.

"What's the hold-up, ladies? We have a lot to do today, and we can't afford any delays." She was clearly irritated but fighting hard to keep a smile on her face. She crossed her arms over her sleeveless black dress and tapped her stiletto on the sidewalk. Jade was about to apologize when Paige began to squeal, jumping up and down on the spot as a taxi pulled up in front of them.

The door opened and Clint Donne stepped out with a suitcase. Jade's heart stopped. He stooped to pay the driver before Paige attacked, pouncing on him as he swung her around. They appeared to be so happy to see each other, but Jade was in too much shock to do anything but stare.

Clint was in New York, in a full cowboy getup—a plaid button-down tucked into his blue jeans, a belt buckle decked with turquoise stones and snakeskin cowboy boots, complete with spurs. To finish the look, he'd pushed back his sandy-blond hair and donned a white Stetson.

"Well, who is this?" he said, looking Jade over with his chocolate-brown eyes. His smooth drawl was something Jade hadn't known she'd missed. "Can't be *my* Jade. This one's way too fancy. And where is she hiding her laptop?" Clint rushed forward, scooping Jade up and bringing her back to reality. Jade laughed and hugged Clint. She really had missed him.

"If you want, we could certainly use a male opinion," Paige said once Clint had put Jade down. She made a grand gesture to the boutique.

"Oh, Paige, this ain't a good idea," Clint said, once he realized where they were. He began to fidget with his suitcase, a nervous look replacing the earlier joy. "It's bad luck for a guy to see the bride in her dress."

"That's the groom, silly." Paige tugged at his sleeve and Clint glared, but Jade was too thrilled by this surprise visit to care. They could fight on their own time.

"I can't believe you're here!" she said. Kindall nudged Jade from behind. "Oh, sorry, this is Kindall. She's our coordinator. Kindall Armstead, meet Clint Donne." When Kindall offered her hand to shake, Clint took it and raised it to his lips, brushing them over her knuckles.

"A pleasure, Miss Armstead."

Kindall's features flushed pink and she gripped her clipboard even tighter. She cleared her throat and composed herself.

"Let's dive right in. Francine is waiting." To Kindall's credit, her voice only trembled slightly. Clint still appeared uncomfortable, but could apparently see that he had no choice in the matter, and followed the women into the shop. Before he could get inside, a wolf whistle sounded out behind them from the street, and Jade watched Clint tip his hat in that direction.

"Got the southern charm turned up to eleven, don't you, cowboy?" Jade asked. Clint smiled at her, but his smile turned to a grimace once he was inside the pink, lacy reception area.

"I did miss you, Jade. It broke my heart when I saw you riding away that morning." Jade picked at the necklace she wore, an old nervous habit she'd thought she'd gotten over years before. "So, tell me more about the new and improved Spencer. I don't remember much about him and the most I've heard from you are complaints." Grateful for the change in topic, but not so much for the subject, Jade complied.

"Turns out he's still a good guy. I was wrong... Well, mistaken about some things. But everything is better now, and I can't wait for you to meet him. He's capable, brilliant and does a lot of charity work." Clint snorted a laugh. "He's a good guy, Clint, and I think you two could get along if you gave him a chance."

"I was there to pick up the pieces after he broke your heart, Jade. Pardon me if I'm not overly eager to shake the man's hand." He looked down at her in a tender way, the kind she hadn't seen since high school. It made her squirm a bit, but she didn't respond. She wouldn't push Clint, not when he'd just arrived. It would be best to ignore it.

"We worked it out, Clint. I promise. But I won't hold it against you if you don't want to meet him. That's up to you."

"Judging by where we are, it looks like the wedding's still on," Clint noted.

Jade could tell Clint wouldn't be backing down anytime soon. She closed her eyes, wishing he would move on so they could enjoy themselves.

"He can't be that good if he's still forcing you to marry him."

"Clint, no one is forcing me into anything. There might not even be a wedding, I'm still not sure. We've been working on the contract and —"

"Wait! There's actually a contract?" he scoffed.

Jade stared at him. *Is he going to act like this the whole time? Why did he even come to New York?*

"He drew up *actual* documentation. *Wow.* What the hell did your parents get you into?" Cint wondered aloud, shaking his head.

Before she could answer, Francine came skipping out of the back room, glowing with something akin to pride.

"Wait until you see what I've got for you," she sang as she yanked Jade to the dressing-room area. Thankful for the diversion, Jade didn't fight her. Paige and Kindall were already in the back, staring at something beside the platform. They parted and allowed Jade to see what it was they were hiding.

The dress hung from a mannequin. A slim bodice clung to the form, all the way down to the hips. From the mid-thigh, it flared out, with wisps of filmy tulle trailing to the floor. Jade stepped closer and saw that the body of the dress was fitted with diamonds over lace that crept up the shoulders. It was sleeveless and champagne in color — everything Jade hadn't known she wanted. She circled around it, where she was met with a dangerous plunge in the fabric along the back.

"It goes with these." Francine directed her to a stand that held a simple rose gold and diamond tiara with matching earrings and necklace. A sheer veil was neatly laid out before her and a box held nude pumps with lace and diamond accents along the sides. Jade was speechless.

"All right, I'll help you into this, and, Paige, why don't you try on your dress?" Kindall said. Jade nodded. *Is this really happening? More than that, am I ready for it?* The honest answer that popped into her head surprised her. She followed Kindall into the changing room and began to ease into the dress.

It appeared to be handmade. No doubt Francine and Candace had spent hours working on the garment alone. The dress fit perfectly, complementing Jade's curves and somehow hiding her imperfections. The V-neck wasn't too low, but, with the back section open, Jade had that hint of sexiness she knew Spencer would appreciate. It was a mix of classic and modern elegance that fit her style to the letter. Kindall zipped her in and added the jewelry. Then she twisted Jade's hair up with a band and fit the veil and tiara into her hair.

"Ready?" she asked. Jade nodded again. She didn't know if she would be capable of speech anytime soon. Francine looked to be on the verge of tears as Jade stepped up onto the platform. When she finally looked in the mirror, she didn't recognize herself. She looked like...a bride. Her head spun and it took all of her strength to stay upright.

At that moment, Paige burst out of her own room wearing a gorgeous burgundy dress with long flowing sleeves and layered skirts. She spun around a couple of times, the gossamer fabric swirling and making her look every bit a medieval princess, before joining Jade on the platform. Kindall brought out a box, this one containing the shoes.

Before she could reach for them, she caught Clint's reflection in the mirror. She had almost forgotten he was there. Normally, when she or Paige would model for him, he'd gag or make some kind of joke. Now, he was eerily quiet, standing a few feet away from the stage. His hat was in his hands and he looked like he was in physical pain. Jade almost asked if he was okay. Then, she saw the flash of a tear run down his cheek. Jade straightened and smoothed the dress.

"It's perfect, Francine, all of it. Thank you." Jade forced a smile for the old woman's sake. It was Jade's dream dress and she definitely wanted more time with it, but right now she was more concerned with Clint. "Will you excuse me?" she asked the women.

Jade hopped down from the platform and grabbed Clint's hand, leading him out of the workshop and into the reception area. No one said a word, and no one tried to follow them. She sat him down in one of the chairs, then sat across from him. "What's going on?"

"Nothing. I wasn't ready, I guess." Clint leaned forward, resting his elbows on his knees as he rubbed his eyes. "I didn't know that *this* is what you would be doing as soon as I showed up." He had a grimace of disgust, as though the dress itself had done something to offend him.

"I'm sorry, but I didn't know you were coming," Jade defended. "If I had, I would have rescheduled this. But I didn't know you would mind." She lowered her voice. "I thought you would be happy for me."

"You don't get it, do you, Jade? I show up, and one of the first things I see is you in a wedding dress," Clint said with a sad smile. "I didn't even want to come in, but you were so… It's like you *want* to marry that creep. I was so stupid, thinking that this was a good idea, thinking I could change your mind. I see now that that's not gonna work."

Oh. So, that's what it is. Jade didn't know how to comfort him, what to say or even if she should try. If she'd known he still had feelings for her, she would have made sure that he never came to New York, much less paraded in front of him in a bridal gown.

"The whole reason I came up here was... It doesn't matter now, does it? I just wanna know if you love him."

"What?" The dress was suddenly constricting Jade's breathing. "I, uh... I think love is a very strong emotion that takes a while to grow."

"You did," Clint deadpanned, "back when we were together. That's why we could never work."

"We both wanted different things, Clint. It wasn't only me." Jade's frustration was building in the form of tears behind her eyes. She wouldn't let him place all the blame for what happened on her. "Yes, I loved Spencer, and I..." She couldn't say it, not like this. Jade pressed her lips together and stared at the floor.

"I would have given up what I wanted if it meant being with you." Clint's solemn tone struck a nerve with Jade. He was here to rescue her, to be the knight in shining armor who would sweep her off her feet and take her back to Texas. As if she needed or wanted that! Her frustration turned to a flooding anger.

"I can't believe you're doing this." Jade's voice came out frigid and distant. "I think you should go to your hotel, Clint. I need a minute to think." She knew that once she was over this, she and Clint would need to talk more, but she couldn't right then.

"Okay." Clint scrubbed a hand over his face. "I'm sorry for my reaction. I shouldn't have said anything." Clint was already standing, hat back on his head. This day had started with so much promise, and now it was all gone.

"I'm staying with Paige while I'm here," he told her. "If you need anything, you know where to find me." He picked up his suitcase from by the door and left her there. Paige stood between the floral curtains wearing a horrified expression. She didn't have to say anything for Jade to know what she was thinking.

"It's fine," Jade assured her. "Neither of us knew how this would affect him."

"He was going to propose to you," Paige blurted. Jade blinked in confusion. "On graduation night when the two of you split up, he had the ring and everything. I swore I'd never tell, but I thought seven years was enough for him to be over you. Jade, I'm so sorry. If I'd thought he still —"

"I thought he was over me, too." Jade swallowed the lump in her throat. Part of her had known back then. That was why they had broken up. Clint had made it clear that he wanted to get married and start a family. Jade had been so focused on her career, and she thought that would be something to consider later on down the line. *Is that why he stayed my friend all these years? Have I been leading him on without realizing?*

Jade sighed and buried her face in her hands, regret beginning to set in. This whole thing was turning into a disaster. Had she lost one of her best friends for good? Cracks were ripping through her heart, but she couldn't break there. She stood up and crossed to the back room. All the women were near the curtains, pretending to be hard at work. Francine and Candace were looking over a dress, while Kindall was writing something down on her clipboard.

Jade couldn't even be mad at them for eavesdropping. She felt like she had been a terrible friend, and all she wanted right now was for someone to tell her everything would be all right and that she had done the right thing. She stomped into the dressing room but caught herself before ripping off the dress. Jade carefully unzipped it and changed back into her old clothes. She removed the veil and jewelry and laid everything neatly on the cushioned bench beside her.

Jade sat alone. She was upset with Clint for not telling her all of this sooner. She was mad at Paige for keeping a huge secret from her. She was terrified that she might very well lose someone important to her. And she was confused, because she realized that she did, in fact, love Spencer.

For the first time in years, Jade allowed herself to simply sit and cry.

Chapter Fifteen

July 29

Jade cursed as hot coffee splashed across her lap before spilling to the floor. The first thing she did was snatch her laptop from her desk before the disaster could destroy it. The second thing she did was carefully stand, place her computer on the bed and head into the bathroom, muttering words that would make her mother gasp if she heard them.

Jade tried to reason with herself that she was upset with the waste of a perfectly good beverage, but she knew that wasn't the case. According to gossip she'd overheard earlier that day, Stacy had been seen inside the building—just what she and Spencer needed. Now it was after nine o'clock at night, Spencer wasn't there and he wasn't responding to any of her texts. Jade had talked herself out of marching down to his office, but it was appealing to her more and more with every tick of the clock.

Jade leaned against the sink, taking deep breaths to calm herself. She trusted Spencer, but she did *not* trust Stacy. The past few days had been hard enough, what with Clint not speaking to her and Paige busy trying to keep him company. Jade didn't know if she and Clint would ever be able to come back from this, and the longer they were out of touch, the more Jade regretted making him leave the way she had.

"But why did he even bother showing up if he was going to pull this stunt?" Jade asked her reflection, practically ripping the buttons off her shirt. She already knew the answer to that. Appalling as it was, Clint's stunt was precisely the reason he was here. He hadn't been kidding about taking her back to Dallas. She tossed her soiled blouse and jeans in the hamper, leaving her in nothing but her white lace undergarments. *First…fresh clothes. Then guy problems.*

Spencer had started leaving his room open to her, since that was where she kept most of her clothes now. It was the same as always when Jade walked in—his bed made tidily, a place for everything and everything in its place. There was a new picture on his nightstand from that day on *The Absolution*. It was one Bryce had taken on his phone of her and Spencer posing in the lounge with enormous smiles on their faces. It brought her back to that day and, for a moment, she felt at peace. Pulling herself from her thoughts, Jade opened the shared closet and walked in, but she didn't go through her clothes.

It had been a temptation from day one, but Spencer was usually with Jade in the mornings when she picked her outfit. She eased over to Spencer's side of the closet and ran her hand over his many hanging suits, all of them almost identical and ranging from black to blue to gray. Then there were his button-down shirts, which hung over a chest of drawers. The shirts were mostly white, but he had a rainbow of other colors behind them. A tie rack with solid colored ties was hanging at the very back.

Without thinking, Jade pulled down one of Spencer's deep blue shirts, one that she recognized as the shirt he'd worn to her welcoming party. She tossed the hanger aside and slipped her arms into the rich fabric, wrapping it around herself. It was well-pressed, but the fabric was still soft. *What the hell's the matter with me?* She ignored the little voice as she buttoned the shirt and told herself it was mere curiosity, perfectly harmless. In reality, it was quite the opposite.

The truth was that Jade was wearing Spencer's shirt because it smelled like his Clive Christian cologne and the color of it mirrored his eyes. Also, though she would never admit it, she missed him and wanted to forget about Stacy and the whole mess she was creating. *Speaking of messes...* Clad only in Spencer's too-big shirt and her socks, Jade found herself back in her room with paper towels and multipurpose spray, scrubbing at the half-dried coffee that covered her desk, chair and floor.

Once her room was spotless, she replaced her laptop on the desk and went downstairs. She was in the hallway when the elevator dinged, and her heart jumped into her throat. Spencer came into the apartment. His tie was loosened and the top buttons of his white shirt were undone, as was usual when he came home. His jacket was draped over his arms, and, judging by how his hair stuck up in places, he or someone else had had their hands all over his head. Jade narrowed her eyes.

"Working hard?" she asked. Spencer snapped around to look at her, and his expression softened. He smiled tiredly at her.

"Sorry I'm late," he said. "Work was insane today."

"Was it?" Jade crossed her arms and leaned her shoulder against the hall. Without a light there, she doubted he could see how upset she was. It wasn't like she wanted to be mad at him, but he had come home late into the night and looking so disheveled that she couldn't help it. All she could see was Stacy climbing all over him and it sickened her. Spencer flung his jacket into the living room, where it landed on the nearest chair.

"What's wrong?" he asked. Jade didn't answer. How could she? Who was she to question his loyalty? As angry as she was and as much as she wanted to accuse him, Jade held back. She wouldn't tell him she was jealous.

"It's not like you to be this late," Jade said in lieu of the truth. She stepped out of the darkness and stood before him. Spencer looked her over appreciatively, but Jade pretended not to notice. She had averted her gaze to the lights beyond the glass. Small streams of rain trickled down the windows, blurring the glowing New York night.

"I know, and I apologized." Spencer stepped closer. "I *am* sorry, Jade."

"Did you hear about Stacy?" Jade asked. Spencer looked surprised. "She was here today. A bunch of people saw her."

"I heard, but what does that have to do with...?" Spencer lowered his head, automatically dropping his hands into his pockets. "I see. Okay, listen to me, Jade. You are annoying and stubborn and it's adorable. But sometimes your one-track mind can get you in trouble. Do you really think I would risk losing you over some woman who I can't even stand to look at?"

"I can't help that I worry." Worry was inaccurate. She was becoming territorial over Spencer, but there was no way he could ever learn that. Jade tugged at the hem of the shirt she wore. Even though the sleeves fell over her hands and the whole thing covered her more than some of the clothes she owned, Jade felt exposed. She hated how accusing she sounded. "I'm sorry. Things are so confusing right now. I don't know who one of my best friends even is, and I certainly don't know what we are to each other. I keep losing control over little things that snowball until I'm at a loss." Jade wanted to stop, but the words kept spilling out faster than she could think them through.

"What do you want?" Spencer stepped forward and placed his large hands on her shoulders. "I know what you're going through, Jade. Trust me. And I want to help you through all of these problems. Let's start with figuring out what *we* mean to each other, because that's important. Know that, at least for my part, you mean more to me than...than everything." He spoke his last word so quietly that Jade almost missed it. She finally looked at him and watched him struggle.

"What do you mean?" she asked, her voice raspy with emotion.

"Jade, I've been falling more in love with you every day that passes." Spencer watched her earnestly. "This is not at all how I wanted this to come up, but there you go. Believe me when I tell you that of all the women in the world, there's no one I'd rather be marrying in a month than you. And, yeah, it's scary, but there it is. I love you, Jade."

Jade turned her head quickly so that Spencer wouldn't notice the color creeping up her cheeks. How long had she wanted to hear that from him? He lifted her chin, forcing her to meet his gaze. He was smiling at her, and Jade knew that he was telling the truth. He did love her. After all this time, after spending years thinking she meant nothing to him... Jade's stomach dropped when she realized that she had never fallen out of love with him in the first place and that ever trying to convince herself otherwise had been foolish.

"You don't have to say anything," he breathed. "In fact, I'd rather you didn't. Like I said before, I'll never ask more than you're willing to give. But I hope that you'll believe me when I say I would never so much as look at anyone else." He bent down to kiss her, a quick motion that struck Jade deeply, resounding through her whole body. When he straightened again, he was smiling at her. "Now, I'm hungry and I'm sure you are. Go pick something to watch. I'll be right behind you."

Spencer pulled his phone from his pocket and began dialing while Jade headed to the sitting room. She was a little lightheaded as her brain tried to process everything that had happened. Jade dropped to the unbelievably comfortable carpet, turned on the television and flipped through programs mindlessly, her thoughts occupied by things that should have terrified her and would have a month before.

Spencer joined her nearly twenty minutes later, wearing red flannel pajama pants and a gray shirt, carrying a takeout bag in his hands. He sat down next to her, placing the bag between them. Jade couldn't look him in the eyes, but she had to. Sure, Jade had every reason to suspect Stacy of bad intentions, but she should have known Spencer wouldn't have given in to her. He had proven himself loyal over the past few weeks in a way Jade hadn't expected.

"I'm sorry I overreacted," she mumbled. "I shouldn't have doubted you like I did. I do trust you, Spence. And…I love you, too." Spencer laughed, grabbing the remote from her hand and clearly enjoying the shocked expression on her face. He leaned across the space between them, his breath hot against her cheek.

"Pride cometh before the fall, Jade Saunders," he warned. Jade swatted him away, her skin tingling.

"How am I prideful? I admitted I was in the wrong."

"You didn't look me in the eyes. In some cultures, that's considered rude." Spencer busied himself with opening the paper bag, hiding the smirk that Jade could hear in his voice. Jade scoffed. *Fine.* If that was how he wanted to play, she would go along with it.

Jade pulled at the collar of the shirt she was wearing, popping it open to display much of her chest and stretching her long legs out in front of her. She noticed Spencer dart his eyes to the motions then back to the bag. *Perfect.* She turned her whole body, pulling her legs behind her, so that she was facing Spencer on her hands and knees. He straightened, swallowing hard as he watched her.

"What are you doing?" he asked softly.

Based on how large the shirt was and how tall Spencer was, even when sitting, he would have a clear point of view down her wide-open collar. Jade's smile widened as she drank in the power that she held over him in that moment.

"Offering a polite and genuine apology," Jade said with mock innocence. She crawled toward Spencer, who didn't move a muscle and watched tight-lipped at the show she was putting on for him. Jade's face was centimeters from his when she said in a sultry tone, "I'm sorry. I should have known better than to doubt you."

"You're playing a very dangerous game, Jade," Spencer said, his voice rumbling in his chest. "Using all...*this* against me like that. A man could get the wrong idea." She was close enough to see that his eyes were darkened and lust-blown and he was tense throughout his entire body. She had the upper hand — just how she liked it.

Jade had started this to push a few of Spencer's buttons, but she hadn't been prepared for it to push a few of hers along the way. Knowing how badly Spencer desired her flipped a switch in her brain. She wanted him, too...and she had him. After all this time, they were each other's.

"Let's make it interesting," Spencer said. Jade realized he'd recovered his senses and all of the power she had held had evaporated. His expression turned predatory, he was no longer at her mercy and she could have sworn she heard him growl. "Tell me when to stop."

Jade's own tactic was turned against her when Spencer raised up, towering over her. She tried to match him but ended up tumbling back and leaning on her elbows, reeling from the shift in dynamic that had taken a second to play out. Spencer was soon caging her with a hand on either side of her shoulders and her legs trapped between his knees. As much as she tried, Jade couldn't keep the smile from her face. Spencer chuckled, his skin so feverish that it threatened to burn Jade more than her own boiling blood could.

"Too much?" he purred, feathering his lips down her throat and across to her exposed shoulder. "Or just enough?" Jade pressed her lips into a thin line and closed her eyes. She wouldn't answer that. She wouldn't give him the satisfaction of knowing what this was doing to her.

Everything up to this point had been flirtatious, even frisky, in comparison. But this was a whole new side to Spencer — and one that she didn't mind. Heat pooled in her core, blazing through her nerves, and she squeezed her thighs together as she damned her body for giving in so easily. Spencer noticed. He ground his hips against her, gliding his fingers up her arm to tangle in her hair as he sought her mouth with a frenzied passion.

"You can tell me to stop whenever you want, Jade," he pulled away just enough to remind her and tugged gently at her black tresses. "I promise to honor my word." *To hell with it*, Jade thought. She threw her arms around Spencer's neck, using him as leverage to press herself up against him. If he was only going to tease her like this, she might as well make her intentions clear.

"Don't stop, Spencer." Though she hadn't meant to, Jade had awoken something within herself — and clearly in him too — something primitive that was a little scary but not unpleasant, and she was determined to explore it further. They were ready. Spencer watched her with astonishment, but a smile quirked at his lips when she repeated, "Don't stop."

Chapter Sixteen

August 1

Jade's limo pulled up in front of The Edison Ballroom. Outside of the tall building, valets rushed back and forth between well-dressed guests, of which there were many. All of them were adorned with glittering jewels, rich fabrics and masks. Jade nervously wrung her black-gloved hands, letting them settle into her lap.

"Miss?" the driver said. "Is everything all right?" Jade nodded but didn't make a move to get out of the car. She took her time, breathing deep and calming her heart rate. *I'm only here for Spencer. I'm only here for Spencer...and Kindall.* Kindall would probably kill her if she bailed on the party.

Earlier that day, Jade had woken up to a note from Spencer that had been stuck to a giant pink box waiting for her in front of their bedroom door. Since their first night together, they had been sharing Spencer's room, so he'd known she would see it. Now that she thought about it, the whole penthouse had started to feel more like home and Jade had even taken to working in the living room rather than cooping herself up all the time.

She had pulled the note from the box and it explained that Spencer had a lot to do, but that he would see her that night at the engagement party. She'd smiled and opened the box, which had turned out to be from Francine and *Timeless Bridal Boutique*.

Jade pushed aside the tissue paper and discovered a dark red ball gown, with a strapless sweetheart neckline and corseted bodice. Layered silk skirts with spiraling threads of silver sparkled throughout the dress, creating a vision of otherworldly beauty. A silvery rose was embroidered over the heart of the dress. She dragged what seemed like miles of fabric out of the box, in awe of Francine and Candace's skill. Then something else fell out.

It was a bag that contained black gloves and a black eye mask. Kindall had come through and, tonight, Jade would have a masquerade ball to attend. She had invited Paige, who'd informed her that she already had her dress, to come over and get ready with her. Clint hadn't said anything, as she'd expected, though Paige did try to get him on the line. Jade wouldn't let him ruin this night for her. She was surprised that he was even still there.

Paige had shown up later, bringing with her a copy of the same pink box. It held a pastel yellow ballgown that had been made with extra tulle and fluff and had similar spirals to Jade's, made of sparkling stones. The sleeves were long, and the neckline came closer to the collarbone, much more in her personal style. Paige's had white gloves and a full-faced white mask with yellow tulips hand-painted on the thin, smooth ceramic.

The two had spent the day together, getting ready side by side and helping each other with hair and makeup, but Paige had left early. She claimed she was needed at the venue to help Kindall with something. Paige had never been a talented liar, and Jade saw right through it. Jade didn't know what her friend was up to, but it probably had nothing to do with Kindall.

Now, as she sat in front of the ballroom, Jade's nerves gripped her in a way that was entirely new. Tonight, she and Spencer would be announcing their engagement to the world. Thankfully, neither of them had been recognized the few times they'd gone out, and they had avoided making any news. *That's going to change come morning.* She checked her makeup and her hair, which she had left to fall in waves down her back. After making sure the heavy eyeliner, smoky shadow and burgundy lipstick were immaculate, she secured her mask then got out of the limo and stepped into an unfamiliar world.

Cameras were flashing in every direction, and she looked around but recognized no one because of their masks. That also meant no one could recognize her, so it wasn't the worst thing. Jade could hear the music and laughter from inside as she stepped up to the velvet rope and lifted her mask enough for the security guards to see her face.

After being ushered inside, Jade was astonished by what she saw. Lights glimmered around her, reflecting from the dazzling chandelier that hung from the ceiling, shining down on the dance floor below. She was on a balcony and, when she leaned against the rail, could see hundreds of people dancing and talking.

Their chatter mingled and echoed in the room, a dull background noise that she found, for the most part, comforted her.

"Ma'am?" A waiter swept a platter before her that held flutes of crisp, bubbly champagne. She took one and thanked the man before finding the stairs that would lead her to the bottom floor. She was sure that was where she would find Spencer and her friends.

Upbeat music flowed from the corner that housed the live band. Jade sipped at her drink. Her dress flowed gracefully around her figure to the floor, and she was definitely drawing some attention because of it. She scanned the crowd, spotting Paige, who was speaking with Kindall and another person. But she couldn't pick Spencer out of the sea of faces.

Jade decided to join her friends for the time being. She wove through the throng, greeting those she recognized, but not lingering. She finally reached Paige and Kindall, who looked amazing in a black evening gown with slivers of gold along the sides and wearing a gold eye-mask.

"Kindall, this place looks magical!" Jade called. Both Kindall and her best friend turned to face her, and Jade saw who she and Kindall had been talking to.

"Clint?" Even with the generic black mask over his eyes and navy-blue tuxedo, she could recognize him anywhere. He smiled awkwardly, casting his glance down to the floor. Jade lifted the mask from her eyes to rest on her forehead. Of course, Clint had been invited, but Jade never thought he'd show.

"You guys probably need to talk," Paige said. "We'll be by the band when you're done." She gave Jade a quick hug, and all but dragged Kindall away from Clint. As much as Jade wanted to talk to him, she wished Paige hadn't run off like that, leaving the two of them alone with nothing but awkwardness between them.

"You look beautiful," Clint said, then cringed as if he regretted his choice of words. "That's probably not what you want to hear from me right now, though, is it?"

"No, it's not." Jade crossed her arms, irritation from the past few weeks replacing the shock of first seeing him. "I've tried to talk to you, to see you, Clint, and you completely shut me off. Why did you even stay here?"

"I know. I'm sorry." Clint grabbed her hands desperately. Jade didn't fight him. "I acted like a selfish asshole, but I didn't mean to hurt you. I'll admit that I had some stuff to work through. I should have done that before I came here, but I was so ready to see you, I didn't think about it. I promise, Jade, that I've been working so hard to move on and be the friend you need me to be."

"You should have done that earlier." Jade wanted to hold on to her anger, make Clint squirm a little, but she couldn't bring herself to do it. "I forgive you. But I swear, Clint Donne, if you pull something like this again, I will kill you."

Clint laughed and pulled her into a bear hug, careful not to spill the flute of champagne still in her hand.

"Easy there, Mr. Donne," the velvety voice that sent a thrill through Jade said from behind them. She looked up into the hypnotizing eyes of Spencer Alexander. He was dressed in a fitted classic black tuxedo with a burgundy vest under his jacket that matched Jade's dress. His hair had been styled straight back from his face and he, too, wore a black mask that was similar to hers. He wasn't smiling, though.

"Ah, you must be Spencer." Clint laughed. "I've heard a lot about you."

"And I you," Spencer said shortly. "Jade, my parents want a word." He offered her his black-gloved hand, and she offered him a glare.

"Sure they do. Sorry, Clint, but can we catch up later?" Clint looked unsure for a moment before nodding.

"That's fine. But…there's something else I need to tell you, but it can wait." He nodded to Spencer then wandered off, getting lost in the sea of masks. Jade pulled her own back down over her face.

"Did you have to be so rude?" Jade scolded Spencer, but she still set her drink down and wrapped her arm around his.

"Rude? I was extremely polite, considering who that was." Spencer began to lead her away, but clearly not to his parents.

"Looks to me like someone was jealous," Jade said. Spencer laughed but didn't deny it. She sort of liked that he was possessive of her. Jade tightened her grip on his arm and leaned into him more.

"I do have some news for you, though, as long as we're talking about parents."

Jade didn't call him out on the subject change.

"Your parents are flying up tomorrow to meet with mine. They tried their best to make it tonight to surprise you, but there were some obstacles, apparently. I wasn't supposed to say anything to you, but I thought you'd like to know. After they see you, we're all getting together to finalize the paperwork. I think you'll like the changes I've made."

"You're kidding!" Jade ignored the last bit he'd said. She had been so wrapped up in everything that it had slipped her mind. "Oh, I can't wait to see them." Spencer smiled, releasing her when he was stopped by an older man. While they talked, Jade thought of how much she had missed her parents. She had been so angry with them when she'd left, but now that she knew they were on their way, she couldn't wait to see them.

"There's something else I want to tell you," Spencer whispered when he was by her side once more. He took Jade's hand and began leading her to the middle of the dance floor, leaning in so that his lips brushed the shell of her ear. "You look dazzling tonight."

Before Jade could respond, she was suddenly pushed from behind. Spencer was able to grab her in time and right her, but several people turned their way. Spencer only checked to make sure she was all right.

"Falling for me in front of everyone," he said. "I'm flattered." Jade laughed, but the snippy comeback she prepared was lost on her tongue. The reason for Jade's stumble was now standing behind Spencer with a smirk.

"Sorry about that," Stacy's high voice sang out. Spencer shut his eyes, probably wishing he had misheard or that he had imagined it. When they both focused all their attention on the other woman, they were disturbed by what they saw.

Stacy was wearing a dress similar to Jade's, only hers was not nearly as lovingly made. It was also apparent that she was wearing bright green contacts that looked a little unnatural. When it was combined with her dyed hair, it was hard to deny what she was doing.

"Why are you here, Stacy?" Spencer stood between her and Jade, blocking Jade's view.

"Despite your best efforts, I'm still a part of New York's most elite. You tried to discredit me, but you didn't reach everyone. Your coordinator invited me, not only to this party, but also to the wedding. Isn't that exciting?" Jade suddenly felt like her dress was laced too tight.

"You haven't yet *seen* my best efforts, Stacy," Spencer growled. He curled his fingers around Jade's arm, pulling her closer to him.

"Is that a fact?" Stacy straightened her mask and crossed her arms, eerily mirroring Jade.

"Stay away from us, Stacy," Spencer warned her quietly. "I mean it." Jade knew there was nothing to be done. It wouldn't do any good to cause a scene here, and that was what Stacy wanted. She could stay for now, but they would have to make sure she was banned from the wedding.

"Don't play into her hands," Jade whispered, pulling Spencer away from the potential mess before them. Stacy wiggled her fingers at them as they walked away.

"I can't believe she's doing this," Spencer mumbled. "I mean, here of all places, knowing full well —"

"Hey, tough guy, dance with me." Jade tried to control the shake that had built in her voice. It seemed that everything about Stacy set her nerves on edge. Spencer didn't seem to be any better off. Thankfully, the music had slowed and the crowd on the floor had thinned. She placed her hands on Spencer's shoulders and began to sway. Spencer gave in, holding her around the waist and moving with her.

It was sort of like a dream for Jade. Though she had grown up in a wealthy household, she had never done anything particularly glamorous. But now, dancing with Spencer, wearing a beautiful ball gown and floating beneath an unreal chandelier, she couldn't imagine things getting any better.

"Jade Saunders," Spencer said. He had cooled down a lot and was now smiling at her. "I love you."

"I know, idiot. Just dance." Jade looked down at their feet. With all those people around, it didn't seem like the time or place. Then again, it *was* their engagement party. "I love you, too," she whispered, not sure if it was loud enough for him to hear. "And I can't wait to marry you."

"Wow." Spencer stilled and stared at Jade with wide eyes. "I think I've finally done it. You're developing...emotions—even expressing them." He laughed when she yanked her hands from his shoulders, and he gathered her up in his arms. "You know I'm joking."

"I know." Jade let him hold her, even when the music died down before stopping completely.

"That being said, I have something for you." Spencer released her and reached into his pocket. "I think, given the circumstances, it's time." He withdrew a small black velvet box, which Jade immediately recognized. Before she could say anything or he could even open the box, the sound of microphone feedback screamed through the room.

"Good evening, everyone," Stacy said into the microphone. That was all it took for Spencer to abandon his mission, shoving the box back in his pocket before beginning to march up to the stage with Jade close behind. "I want to start by congratulating our guests of honor, Jade and Spencer." A round of applause went up through the crowd and Jade finally caught up to and slowed Spence.

"Let go, Jade," he said. "I don't know what she's going to do, but this has to stop. I won't let her take thi—"

"With that out of the way, I have an announcement," Stacy continued. Spencer turned to the stage, frozen to the spot. But Stacy wasn't watching him. She was looking dead into Jade's eyes when she said, "Spencer, darling, I'm pregnant."

Chapter Seventeen

August 2

Jade's ears were still ringing as she sat on the penthouse's staircase. Stacy's mouth was moving, but Jade couldn't for the life of her hear what was being said. Stacy had just arrived, now dressed in an oversized purple sweater and dark leggings. There wasn't a black hair out of place, and she didn't look like she'd lost any sleep. Spencer, on the other hand, looked terrible.

He was seated in a chair, staring out of the windows at the foggy morning and dim city lights, nursing a glass of strong-smelling amber liquid. He still wore his clothes from the night before, only now they were slightly more wrinkled. The jacket and vest lay next to him, and his hair fell over his forehead, probably limp from the repeated running-through of his hands.

"Thought you could get rid of me, didn't you?" Stacy sneered, looming over Spencer, waving a manila folder in front of his face. "Use me up and throw me out, huh? It won't work now."

"Back off, Stacy. You're the only one using people," Bryce said from where he was perched on the kitchen counter. He'd gone home with Spencer and Jade, and stayed up with them all night, so he was also still in his tux. "If it weren't for that folder you've got shoved in Spencer's face, I would think this was something you'd done for publicity."

"What are you even doing here?" Stacy straightened, hands on her hips and abnormally green eyes glaring at the youngest Alexander.

"I'm here to support my brother, unlike you, you pathetic hag."

Stacy threw her hands in the air, dropping herself into the nearest chair and tossing the folder onto the end table next to her.

Bryce went on. "What the hell were you even thinking, announcing something like that at a very public event? You had no right!"

"No, *he* had no right," she said, jabbing a perfectly manicured finger in Spencer's direction. "I tried to contact you, Spencer, but you ignored me. I tried to come by and see you in person to tell you, and you turned me away, even at the party. Jesus, did you think that nothing would happen? There was a reason I stayed in contact with you, tried to build a relationship. It wasn't all PR!"

"I don't remember much about that night," Spencer said. They were his first words that morning, and they were spoken in a raspy voice with a dangerous calm. "Stacy, I was dead drunk and you knew it. That's the only reason any of this happened in the first place."

Stacy reared back, ready to release her outrage on Spencer, when Jade stood from where she had been sitting on the stairs. She, too, had remained silent, but now she had to do something.

"Guys, we all need to take a breath, okay? It's been a stressful morning for everyone." She straightened her shirt, vowing that she would keep a cool head through all of this. No one argued with her. Since the press had been there the previous night, Stacy's 'news' had been splattered all over the papers. This was the Alexanders' first real scandal, more than rumors in a gossip rag, so it wouldn't be dying down any time soon.

"Why are you even still here, Jade?" Stacy taunted. "Haven't you gone home yet?"

"You don't speak to her like that." Spencer put his glass down and came to stand beside Jade. "Say whatever you want to me, but she's not part of this."

"As your fiancée, I'd say she's a bigger part than Bryce."

Bryce huffed from the kitchen at that.

"You can't abandon this baby, Spence. Not now. All this could have been avoided if you had talked to me."

"I'm through, Stacy. You had your chance. You could have asked to speak to me privately at the engagement party instead of shoving Jade, and you didn't. You wanted this to happen."

Stacy stood up, stomping over to Spencer and Jade, standing as close to them as she could. Bryce hopped down from the counter, clearly readying himself in case he needed to intervene.

When Stacy didn't say anything, Spencer continued, "There was no reason to humiliate me and my family the way you did."

"You're right, and I am sorry." Stacy's voice trembled along with her bottom lip.

Jade couldn't believe what she was seeing. *Does she think that's convincing?* Spencer obviously didn't buy it either and stared at her blankly.

"Blame it on hormones!" Stacy finally shouted. "I was hurt and lonely, Spence, because of what you did." She reached up to try to touch him, but he took a step back.

"I think it's best if you leave," Spencer said. "For the time being, I've unblocked you, so you can get in touch with me any time. I'll let you know when it's best to come back."

Stacy looked between him and Jade. She scoffed, turning on her heel and grabbing her jacket.

"I'll be back in an hour," she muttered, pressing the elevator button. "If you don't let me in, I'll be more than happy to let everyone know what kind of father you are." She turned to them with a smirk. "Oh, and Spence? I don't want Jade to be here when I get back. Bryce either. It's clear that we need some alone time to talk about our future." The way she said 'alone time' made Jade grind her teeth together to keep herself from saying something she might regret.

As soon as Stacy had gone, Spencer collapsed back into his seat. He ran his hands through his dark brown hair for the tenth time that hour, making it stand up in places even more. The bags under his dulled eyes tugged at Jade's heart.

She wanted to help him, to support and comfort him. She wasn't mad at Spencer. How could she be? He hadn't asked for this. But she was in a dilemma herself. She had started to trust him again, had fallen in love and was ready to marry him, but this put a crack in the bridge they had worked so hard to repair. Should she step aside and let Stacy into their life? What did Spencer want to do? Jade wiped her sweaty palms on her jeans as she sat across from Spencer.

"Don't ask me," he said, not meeting her gaze. "I've thought of nothing else and I still don't know what to do."

"Stop reading my mind," Jade teased. She was hoping to draw a smile out of him, but she only got a weak snort, devoid of humor.

"I'm sorry I put you in this position." Spencer finally looked at Jade. "I should have been more careful. I should have known something like this would happen. She was a problem before you showed up. I don't know why I thought that would change."

"Don't apologize to me, Spence. How are your parents holding up?" Spencer shrugged, and Bryce took over.

"They're not happy, but they're managing." Bryce came over to put a hand on Spencer's shoulder. "They're not blaming you, Spencer. They know this was one hundred percent Stacy's doing. The real question is...what is her end goal?"

"I think..." Jade trailed off. She hadn't wanted to say anything earlier, but since Stacy hadn't held back when she'd been there, Jade wouldn't either. "I think she wants me gone. She wants to marry Spencer and never see my face again."

"To me, it looks more like she wants to *be* you." Bryce sat on the arm of Spencer's chair. "She's become unhinged. Anyone can see it."

Spencer was unfocused, his drink back in his hand with a significant amount missing. Bryce took the glass from him, and he didn't protest.

"So, where do we go from here?" Jade asked.

"I need to be held responsible for my actions," Spencer whispered. "I have to do what's right."

"You can't mean —?" Bryce spoke up.

"Even though Stacy is the mother, I am the father of this baby and there's no getting around that. I'll be there for Stacy and our child." Jade's heart dropped into her stomach. She'd been afraid he'd say that, so it wasn't unexpected. "Jade?"

"I need time to think." Jade stood up, the sounds around her muted in her ears. Spencer had jumped up, taking her hands in his. He was saying something, but Jade didn't hear. She had adjusted to life with Spencer, even looking forward to their future. She had always loved him, even when he'd hurt her. And being with him again only made that more obvious, even if she'd never said anything. And now, once again, the rug had been pulled out from under her.

"Jade, what do you mean?" Spencer's worried voice finally reached Jade and she blinked. "I'm not saying I want to give up what we have."

"I know." Jade finally registered that he was holding her hands and she squeezed. "But we all know that Stacy is going to try everything in her power to make that happen. The three of us could never work it out. And I won't risk her hurting you or your child for anything. We'll need to think of other options, but for now, you have to let me go, Spencer. I want to see my parents. I want to see Paige and Clint." For the first time ever, Spencer looked like he was about to cry, and Jade didn't think she could stand to watch that. She raised up on her toes and planted a small kiss on his cheek.

"Bryce, take care of him, okay?" Jade grabbed her phone and wallet from the counter, then her jacket from the chair. "I'll be in touch. I promise." She stopped before calling the elevator. She couldn't leave like this. Jade turned, threw her arms around Spencer and kissed him hard. "We'll figure this out. I promise." Now, she could leave.

She boarded the elevator, still not looking at the Alexander brothers. She checked her phone for the first time since the previous night. She had dozens of notifications, missed calls and texts. She turned the screen off. Her parents wouldn't arrive until that afternoon. She knew that much. But where could she go now?

* * * *

Paige answered the door after only one knock. Still in her pajamas with her wheat-colored hair wild on her head, she leaped onto Jade, latching hard. She didn't say anything, but still managed to seem more upset than Jade was.

"I'm fine, Paige," Jade said in a steady voice. "Where is Clint?"

"Making breakfast," Paige said. She was by no means a morning person — never had been — and it was evident by her drooping eyes. Jade appreciated Paige waking up early for her sake. It was a nice hotel room, with a sitting area, a full kitchen and more rooms branching off. Clint was in said kitchen, pushing eggs around in a skillet. Jade smiled as Paige fell onto the couch. She could imagine her friend would be blissfully unaware of what happened around her as she closed her eyes in a likely attempt to doze off again.

"Morning," Jade said to get Clint's attention. He hummed an acknowledgment, also still in pajamas, but he didn't face her. "Is everything all right?"

"Not really," Clint said. "I was actually going to call you later, but I figured you were busy. We need to talk."

"Look… If you want to say, 'I told you so' or anything about Spencer being a bad guy, save your breath, because I don't want to hear it." Jade settled onto one of the bar stools and rested her chin on her hand. Clint finally looked at her, setting the pan of cooked eggs on a potholder nearby.

"That's not what I was going to say at all." Clint rubbed his hands together nervously. "I wanted to talk to you about Stacy."

"What about her?" Jade asked. "I take it you've read the papers. What more is there to say?"

"I know her." The air was sucked from Jade's lungs with that and, once she recovered, she had to ask Clint to repeat himself. "Stacy was the one who told me to come here, Jade. She sent me the plane ticket and everything. And I was stupid enough to trust her. Do you want something to drink?"

"What? No! I want you to explain yourself right now, Clint." Jade was seeing red. *What did Stacy do? Is this whole thing some plan to get back at Spencer?*

"After I got your email when you first got to New York, I got another message from Stacy on social media. She introduced herself as Spencer's girlfriend. She told me that all of you were unhappy with this arrangement and that the only way to fix it was for me to come up here and rescue you. She was the one who convinced me to tell you about my true feelings."

"But, you didn't 'rescue me'. In fact, you've barely spoken to me since that day at the bridal shop." Jade's mind was reeling. Who could she trust anymore?

"Well, no. You were the happiest I'd ever seen you, and I couldn't try to take you away from that. I ignored you for a long time because I was trying to sort out my own thoughts." Clint threaded his fingers through his sandy hair. "I realized that you weren't mine anymore, Jade, and that I had no reason to be here, other than support my friend. It was long past time to move on, so I started focusing on that. I knew I couldn't do it around you, though. I still felt guilty for the reason I'd come here in the first place. Then Stacy stopped talking to me and I assumed she'd backed off. When I saw her at the party, though, I got suspicious and — "

"Stacy has been trying to split Spencer and me up from the very beginning." Jade absorbed this new information. "And she tried to use one of my friends to do it." Something was missing, though. A key piece of the story still needed to be told, but Clint didn't have it. Only Stacy could finish the puzzle. Seeing the near-depressed look on Clint's face, Jade decided to help him out. After all, he had been lied to and manipulated by Stacy, too.

"Thank you for telling me," she said, resting her hand on top of his clenched fist. He relaxed, his expression softening. "I know how hard that must have been, but it means a lot."

"You could pay me back, you know." Clint looked up at her with a sly smile. Jade laughed, and it felt damn good to do it.

"Pay you back? Wow. Assuming I would, what would you want?"

"How about that cute little party planner's number?" he asked with a wink. "I'm a new man now and I think I'd like to talk to her a little more."

"Kindall is an event coordinator who would kill you if she heard you call her a party planner." Jade sighed and pulled out her phone. "I'll see what I can do, I guess."

"Some of us are happily single and trying to sleep over here," Paige groused, putting a hold on their conversation. Paige was small, but if anything came between her and her sleep, there were dire consequences.

As Jade was typing out a message to Kindall, a light bulb went off over her head. She quickly sent the text, then opened her browser, typing in a few choice words. Maybe Stacy didn't hold the final piece at all. Maybe Jade had to be the one to find it.

Chapter Eighteen

The penthouse was empty when Jade returned home. She wasn't sure if that was good or bad but decided that, for the moment, it served her purpose. She had spent her day at the Park Terrace Hotel, devising a plan with Paige and Clint, then making one very important call that would set the dominoes tumbling. It wouldn't be easy and she didn't know if Spencer would approve, but she was sure she knew how to fix the Stacy situation.

For now, she had dinner plans with her parents at Gramercy Tavern to worry about. Their plane had landed and they had, of course, heard of last night's catastrophe but weren't saying much over the phone. Instead, they had invited her out to eat with them after they got settled, which was code for 'we have questions, and you have answers'.

Jade went upstairs to get ready, still walking quietly in case Spencer was in his room. She even rapped on the door before entering, but there wasn't anyone there.

Jade briefly wondered where Spencer was. She knew that Bryce had gone home for the evening, but Spencer hadn't replied to her, so he could be out with Stacy right now and she would be none the wiser. For some reason, she hated the idea of the two of them being seen in public together. People would talk even more, and Stacy could use that to force Spencer into doing whatever she wanted.

As Jade sifted through her dresses, she contemplated her situation. She didn't like lying to Spencer, but she needed to protect him. Besides, it wouldn't be lying, only not sharing her plan with him. And if it turned out that she was wrong, bringing him in would only hurt and confuse him. For now, she would keep it between her and her friends and hope to God she was right. Still, there was that nagging voice in her head admonishing her and telling her to be honest with Spencer.

Jade shook her head and selected a simple, short-sleeved white dress with a black satin band around the middle and black lace along the skirt's hem. She paired it with white heels and pulled her hair up into a ponytail. It was just dinner with her parents, after all, but it wasn't for a little while — and she had work to do.

Jade's first stop was the kitchen. There, on the counter, she found the folder Stacy had left behind. Spencer must have looked through it because the pages were shoved in haphazardly. She flipped it open and looked over the doctor's report of a positive pregnancy test. She knew this wasn't meant for her eyes, but her need to know the truth was screwing with her morals. She inspected the document closely, looking for any sign of tampering or falsification. There was nothing that she could see.

Jade was back upstairs in a flash, standing before Spencer's office door. She'd been given his permission to enter and use whatever she needed, but it still felt like an intrusion, considering the folder she was holding tightly against her midsection. She decided to go for it, swinging the door wide and marching over to the scanner. Jade turned the machine on and made copies of all the documents, each second that ticked by feeling like an eternity. Spencer could walk right in without warning. She was sliding the copies into her bag when her phone rang. Jade jerked, scattering the contents of her bag across the floor. Luckily, her laptop was still safely in the sitting room.

Jade pulled out her phone and checked the ID. *Spencer.* "Hello?" she answered.

"Jade, hi." She could hear traffic in the background, so she knew he was outside. Jade bent over to collect her things and stuffed them back into the bag. When she didn't reply right away, he continued, "Where are you right now?"

"At the house. Why?" It was impossible to tell if he was alone, but she hoped he was. She closed her eyes, upset with herself at acting so possessive.

"I was wondering what your plans were for tonight." His tone was hushed, and she could guess that Stacy was there with him. She rolled her eyes, standing and slinging her bag onto her shoulder.

"Dinner with my parents. After that, I don't know." She didn't try to hide her irritation, unfounded as it was. She was being petty, sure, but she also didn't need Stacy stalking her anymore. Why had he gone out with her? Wasn't he aware of the hundreds of people out there with phones, waiting to add fuel to the fire that his life was becoming? All it would take was one photo and things would become much worse.

"We need to talk, Jade. Will you be home tonight?"

"I should be." She leaned against the wall, fiddling with her necklace again. Her suspicions were confirmed when she heard that familiar, squeaky tone from somewhere in the background of the call. Anger began to bubble beneath Jade's calm demeanor and a small crack allowed it to leak out. "I have to go, Spencer. Don't keep Stacy waiting, okay?"

"I'm not… That's not what —"

"I'll see you tonight. Bye." Jade hung up before he could say anything, taking a shuddering breath and closing her eyes. She had to stop letting her emotions control her. It would only cause more problems. She knew Spencer felt bad enough as it was and she was only hurting him more. He didn't deserve that. Jade tossed the folder back where she'd found it, trying her best to make it look the way Spencer had left it, then checked the time on her phone and cursed. If she didn't leave now, she would be late. It was less than a ten-minute drive with traffic, but she wanted to get there before they did.

Gramercy Tavern was a homey restaurant, with contemporary designs of black and white. There wasn't a huge crowd that night, but there was the dull buzz of conversation around her. She spotted her parents, already seated at a table near the wall. Like her dad always said, *'If you're on time, you're late'*. Jade smiled at the sight of her family. She gave her name and was shown to their table.

"Hey, you!" Jade's mom leaped from her seat to wrap her arms around Jade. Timothy stayed in his seat but grinned up at his daughter.

"It's been a while, pumpkin."

Jade sat next to her father and gave him a hug. She didn't want to let go. It had only been a month, but she'd felt their absence, especially now, when things were at their worst.

"I missed you guys. Even if we have been working together, you're still a million miles away."

Timothy chuckled and took a sip of water then said, "See? And I bet you learned that things are a lot different when you don't have me around to help you out." He set his glass down and turned to Jade, his hands clasped before him. "Speaking of which, tell us all about this mess your fiancé got himself into."

"Dad," Jade said, fixing her eyes on her lap.

"Tim, stop," her mother spoke at the same time. "We haven't been here five minutes and you start in."

"You're thinking it, too, Angela," he said. "We're going to have to have this conversation one way or the other, and I'd much rather get it out of the way, wouldn't you?"

He'd made a fair point. Jade took a huge gulp of her own water.

"If you've read the reports, you already know everything," she said. "There's not much more to it, and Spencer and I are going to talk more about it tonight." *I hope.* "Everything is under control, Dad."

"I, for one, wouldn't believe a word this Stacy girl said," Timothy said, "not until I had concrete proof."

"Spencer does. Sort of..." Jade thought about the copies she had stowed away in the bag at her feet. "I think the most important thing right now is to act like adults about the whole...situation. It doesn't have to be this dramatic incident that it has turned into. In my opinion, everyone could have handled things a little better, but most of all Stacy."

"I agree," Angela said. She raised her wineglass. "I am proud of you, Jade. You've had a lot thrown at you in a short time, but you're handling it all so well. I know you'll make the right decisions." She smiled at her daughter, who smiled in return. If only Angela knew that deep down inside, Jade was screaming.

Once the unpleasant topic was out of the way, Jade enjoyed the visit with her parents and was in better spirits by the time she got home. The two glasses of wine had given her a fuzzy feeling, and the delicious food had filled and comforted her. She kicked off her heels and they landed somewhere in the hallway. Jade walked across the warm marble floors to the windows, watching the lights flash across the horizon.

"You look nice," Spencer said from the hall. Jade ignored his compliment, not the least bit surprised by his presence, and she turned to sink onto the couch that faced the window.

"And you wanted to talk," she countered. "So talk."

"Have you been drinking?" Spencer asked as he came to stand in front of her.

"Not enough to do any damage," she said without thinking. She watched the pain flicker over Spencer's face and winced. "I'm sorry. I meant —"

"I know what you meant," Spencer said. "It's okay." He sat next to her, close but not touching. Jade noted that he had showered recently and changed into sweats and a T-shirt. "The real question is, are *you* okay?"

"I wish you would stop asking that," Jade groaned.

"I know you're not happy with the arrangement between Stacy and me, but we can all make this work."

"I'm fine with it. It's just that my moral compass is a little off course, Spence. Nothing to do with you..." Spencer gave her a look that clearly said he didn't believe her. Finally, Jade caved. "I know you want to do the right thing, and I'm glad you do. Then there's this selfish part of me that wishes you wouldn't. Part of me wants none of this to be real and—" Jade stopped herself before she could reveal that she was trying to *prove* none of this was real. She had to stop misplacing her anger at Stacy onto Spencer. It wasn't fair to him. He was doing the best he could with the bad hand he'd been dealt.

"That's normal, Jade," Spencer said. Jade breathed a sigh of relief that he hadn't caught on to her almost-slip. "Hell, even I've wondered if Stacy is telling the truth." Jade perked up at that. Then something occurred to her. What if Spencer had already taken it upon himself to find out if Stacy was lying? That would explain why he would spend time with her, making her think she was safe. Perhaps, like her, he'd even gone to a professional. "It seems like something she would try. If it hadn't been for those papers she brought over..."

If it was true that Stacy was suspect enough to make Spencer doubt her word—and she most certainly was—then she could bring him in on the scheme. What was the worst that could happen? Jade weighed her choices carefully, taking five full beats of silence to decide before determining that it was worth the risk.

"What if she faked the documents?" Jade asked. Spencer didn't put much stock into her question and shrugged tiredly. If he had thought it, he hadn't acted yet. That was a promising sign. "I'm serious, Spence. It's not that hard to do. And people do this sort of thing all the time."

"A fake pregnancy wouldn't do her any good," Spencer rationalized, now piercing her with his stare. "Even if she did, it would show within a few months."

"Which would be enough time to call off the wedding and isolate us from each other." She thought about telling him Clint's role in all of this but knew that it would further complicate matters. She would tell him later. Jade snatched up her bag and grabbed the pages still stuffed in there, no longer worried about Spencer finding out she had been snooping. Spencer, in turn, didn't ask why she had them. He only moved closer to her to read along with her.

"It's so easy these days to look up what positive results should look like—and even easier to copy them." Jade flipped through the pages. "Don't be angry, but I talked it over with my friends, and they thought we should hire a private investigator, someone with the authority to look further into this."

"That's not a bad idea. I don't think any would be available at this hour, but I'll try in the morning." Spencer pulled out his phone, but Jade put a hand over his screen.

"I'm glad I hired one earlier, then." Spencer froze, turning to look at her in disbelief. "Please, don't be mad." Spencer put his phone away, a small smile tugging at the corner of his lips.

"While I do wish you had discussed it with me first, I'm not mad. In fact, I think it's sweet in a...twisted way." He threw an arm around her and pulled her close. "But I need you to understand that if this turns out to be real, we'll have to deal with it...together."

"I know," she said. "I didn't tell you because I was angry and confused. And, yes, I was taking it out on you, which wasn't fair. If it turns out she's telling the truth, I'll apologize to her and live with whatever choice you make. I promise."

Spencer tilted her chin up to look into her eyes.

"Whatever choice *I* make? Jade, you should know that, no matter what, I choose you. I'll help her with our child, but I'll still be married to you — if you want me, that is." Jade pretended to ponder his question before lifting herself from the couch to kiss him deeply.

"I think I'll keep you, baby or not." They sat there, content to be in each other's arms. Spencer kept his hand on Jade's shoulder, rubbing circles on her sleeve with his thumb. Then, Jade thought of something. "Speaking of earlier, where were you when I came by to get ready?"

"Stacy demanded we go out to dinner together," Spencer said. "And, before you find out the hard way, she's going to be coming by again tomorrow."

"That's fine. In fact, let's keep it that way. I want Stacy close for the next few days." Jade glared at the wall in front of her, causing Spencer to huff a laugh.

"That didn't sound sinister at all," Spencer said sarcastically. Jade poked his rib and he laughed. "I know what you meant — and don't worry. I'll keep her entertained while your private eye checks her story."

"I can't believe you're on board with this." Jade shifted her focus so that her eyes were fixed on a distant, blinking red light outside. It was slowly hypnotizing her into a drowsy state. Spencer pressed his lips to her hair.

"I don't trust her, either, Jade. But I sincerely hope you're wrong. If Stacy is willing to go to these lengths, I'm afraid of what else she might do."

Jade agreed. For now, though, in Spencer's arms, with his steady breathing and the blinking light, Jade wanted to sleep. She turned to tell him as much, but Spencer had already nodded off beside her.

Chapter Nineteen

August 5

It was late afternoon when Jade boarded the elevator. She was dressed in her sharpest black pantsuit, with her hair and makeup professionally done. Since the original meeting had been postponed, the Alexanders and Saunders were meeting today to finalize the buyout and...other details.

Jade and Spencer had spent a chunk of the morning on the phone with Dylan Hancob, and the private investigator had assured them that with the generous payment they'd offered, he would have answers for them before the day was over.

Things were going right for the first time since the engagement party. Jade felt like she had regained control of a swerving vehicle in the nick of time, but the tightness remained in her chest and she was sure it wouldn't go away until everything was resolved. Hopefully, this meeting would relieve some of the pressure. The elevator doors opened to a floor of offices. It was filled with the sounds of conversation, ringing phones and clacking keyboards. Jade passed the cubicles briskly, aiming for the glass office at the other side. The whole floor and office layout was a mirror image of where she herself worked, only Spencer's furniture seemed to be made of glass and metal. *How fitting.*

Jade could see Spencer hunched over his sleek, brushed-silver desk, reading something on his monitor. She smiled, tapping lightly on the window to get his attention.

"Come in," he called without looking up. Jade slipped through the door and laughed.

"You know, when I thought about your office, I imagined some big, intimidating executive monstrosity with bookshelves and a TV. Not this." Spencer glanced up at the sound of her voice and gave her a half-smile.

"I like my people to have access to me," he said. "And seeing them hard at work motivates me to do my best by them." He closed out of his work and straightened up. "Are you ready?"

"As I'll ever be," Jade replied.

Spencer grabbed a folder from his desk and gestured for Jade to lead the way. The infamous knot once again wound itself into her gut. She knew that one floor down, both of their parents were waiting for them in a conference room.

Spencer didn't say anything before they got there. Jade couldn't even get a read on how he was feeling, which served to make her even more nervous. She had held many conferences in her years at Saunders' Metalwork, but this one wouldn't even be in the same ballpark. This would change everything. *Today* would change everything.

The room Spencer took her to turned out to be much like the rest of the building. With a smart, modern feel and floor-to-ceiling windows, the room was flooded with natural light, illuminating the empty chairs. They stopped in their tracks.

"Weren't they supposed to be here?" Jade asked.

"I'm not worried," he said, opening the door for her. "After all, this isn't some formal meeting with attorneys and board members. We're not giving them marks for punctuality." Clearly, Spencer could tell she was nervous. Jade stuck her tongue out at him, and he laughed. He tossed his folder on the table and took a seat in one of the chairs across from her.

"I'm ready to get this over with," Jade said quietly.

"Do you mean with the meeting or the deal with Mr. Hancob?" Spencer asked, leaning far back in his chair with his hands clasped behind his head. Jade didn't answer. She hated how easy it was for him to know what she was thinking, so she decided it would be best not to say anything at all.

Time ticked by and, a few minutes later, the Alexanders and her parents exited the elevator together. Jade assumed they had all gone to lunch to catch up before the meeting. It brought back memories of when she had been younger, when she would wait up, despite what the babysitter said, to see her parents coming home from their nights out with the Alexanders. She had always thought Victoria Alexander was the most glamorous woman and that she could never be like her.

"Sorry we kept you waiting," Carlton said, immediately getting to the point. "But we're here now and I'm sure we all know what we want. So, let's get started." They all took seats, Carlton and Victoria next to Spencer and Timothy and Angela on either side of Jade.

"First of all, this acquisition is happening, with or without the marriage," Timothy said. "We've already decided that much." Spencer's parents nodded in agreement.

"Good. But you should know that the marriage is on," Jade said, earning a raised eyebrow from her father. Even Spencer looked taken aback by Jade's authoritative tone. He smiled and leaned back to make himself comfortable, obviously glad to let Jade take the reins.

"Spencer kindly offered to have the marriage be on paper alone, but I think we need to go ahead and admit that it doesn't matter." Jade stood from her chair and began to walk around the room, commanding the attention of everyone present. "This should never have been about a marriage or a scandal. This is about two companies coming together, handing off the baton to the next generation and allowing those who have worked all their lives a chance to take it easy for once." She gave Timothy a soft smile. "And now, it's evolved into two people who love each other. I say we forget about what brought us here and focus on the future."

"I agree," Victoria said. "I admit that it didn't make sense in the beginning, but I went along with it because, well, it's how I met Carl. But times have changed, and we should change with it."

"Still, I am glad that it happened the way it did," Spencer said. "I could have done without the Stacy situation, but the one good thing is that I have my second chance with Jade and I'm not going to screw it up again." Spencer opened the folder he had brought with him and took out four copies of the same sheet. He gave one to Jade and the others to the CEOs, keeping one for himself. "That being said, I took the liberty of reworking the original agreement. I think you'll find this a little more to your liking," he added to Jade. She took a seat next to him.

The new contract had nothing about a marriage or even about Jade being given an executive position. Instead, at the very bottom, it stated that upon Alexander International's acquirement of Saunders' Metalwork, Jade would be given full control over her father's company, as she had been promised when she was younger. Spencer would, of course, take over AI and check in on Jade's work now and again. The metalworking company would still be owned and used by Alexander International but would operate independently.

"Is this real?" Jade asked, hardly able to contain her enthusiasm.

"It's what you were born to do," Spencer said. Carlton and Timothy scanned over the papers, clearly approving of the work Spencer had put into them.

"Everything seems to be in order here. But, before we sign, there is another matter to be discussed." It was Carlton's turn to stand now. "I love you, but I want to make sure you have everything under control, Spence. Your choices will now impact this company directly. That being said, what are you going to do about Stacy?"

Spencer leaned back in his chair and thought a moment before he answered.

"My mistakes are my own and I will take responsibility for them," he said. "Jade is the woman I love and will marry, but I will also not abandon my child. You should also be aware that right now there is a Mr. Hancob who is looking into the validity of her statements, so this might not even be an issue. Either way, I don't think this will hinder my ability to run my company."

"And you, Jade? You agree with this?"

Jade nodded.

"All right." Satisfied with both of their answers, Carlton sat back down with a content smile on his face. "I trust you, Spencer."

"Sounds to me like the only thing left to do is sign these papers," Timothy said, producing a pen from the inner pocket of his suit. He winked at Jade and began scribbling his name on the blank lines. The rest of them followed suit until all the proper lines showed the proper signatures. Carlton and Spencer stood, the older man offering his hand to his son. Spencer took it, a grin splitting his face.

"You take full ownership in October, Spence." He gathered the documents and laid them in his briefcase. "I'll get these to the lawyers, where they will be notarized and filed, and we're done." Carlton's eyes shone with pride for Spencer. "I think you'll be all right." As Victoria wrapped her arms around Spencer, Jade's mom embraced her.

"Are you sure you're ready to get married?" she asked.

"Mom, you know me," Jade answered. "I would never agree to something that I wasn't prepared for." Timothy joined in on the hug.

"Given recent events, I can't say I approve one hundred percent," he muttered. "But as long as you're happy, sweetheart." It wasn't until after their parents had boarded the elevator that Jade and Spencer allowed themselves to express their excitement. Jade began to laugh, unable to believe what had happened. Spencer cut her off, sweeping her against him and kissing her deeply.

"We did it," he whispered. "I told you that nothing could get in our way."

"I knew you were right." Jade threw her arms around his neck and pecked his lips. "I just didn't want it going to your head. Why didn't you tell me you had rewritten the contract? We talked about this last night and you didn't say a word."

"I thought it would be a nice surprise. Was it not?"

"It was definitely a surprise." Jade laughed.

"With the way you were handling things in there, I'm sure you would have demanded it at some point." He gave her a sly smile. "I do love a woman who takes control." Jade blushed at the comment, even though she should have been used to it by now. She wondered if she would ever get used to Spencer Alexander.

"So, how should we celebrate?" she asked, desperate for a subject change. Spencer looked like he wanted to continue with his original train of thought, but he gave in.

"We could go to the park," he suggested. "Just the two of us? Get out of this office and enjoy a little fresh air."

"You don't have plans?" Jade put emphasis on her last word, to which Spencer shrugged.

"Not yet," he said. "In fact, I haven't heard from Stacy at all today. It's not the worst thing that could happen, but I am a bit worried." He tapped his fingers on the back of a chair. "I'm sure she's fine, though. And I won't let her spoil *this* for us. We've earned it, I think." Jade nodded in agreement.

Stacy's out-of-character silence was alarming, especially in her condition. But Spencer had a point. They couldn't put their lives on hold because she hadn't texted in a few hours. Stacy had taken up so much of Spencer's time lately that Jade had started to feel left out. And they did deserve this. Before the next year, they would be partner CEOs of one of the largest corporations in America.

"Madame," Spencer said, offering his arm to Jade. She looped her arm around his and together they boarded the elevator. When they got outside, Jade was surprised when there wasn't a black car waiting for them. Before she could ask, Spencer answered, "Bryant Park is only a block or so away."

It was a warm, breezy August afternoon. A few clouds dotted the sky, but the sun still shone brightly. He was right. The sidewalks were somewhat crowded and the streets were congested with traffic, but Jade was glad to be out of the office, out of the penthouse and out in the world.

Before long, Jade and Spencer came to the park, where they found a small trail tucked away in a grove of trees. The leaves had started turning yellow and orange, with the occasional leaf floating to the path before them. Spencer began tugging her farther down the trail until they reached an isolated little opening that housed a single fountain. Spencer and Jade sat on the edge, the sounds of trickling water and chirping birds mingling with the chaos the city that wasn't as far off as it seemed.

"So," Jade started, crossing her arms and sighing. "The wedding is officially on, huh? That'll be fun."

"And since it's in September, it'll give us time for the honeymoon before we start working." Jade wanted to say something, to push it off until the first of the year. It was too soon, so would cause a lot of unnecessary stress and be hard enough to pull off, even with all the money in the world. But before she could voice it, she realized that she didn't want to argue this. Kindall had already been pushing herself to plan this wedding, and she would be devastated if it were postponed, even for a day.

Jade's phone suddenly went off in her pocket, the tinkling music-box tone slicing through the quiet atmosphere. Her eyes widened, as did Spencer's. She quickly dug the phone from her jacket and checked the caller ID. It was Dylan. She pressed accept, holding the phone to her ear.

"Hello?"

"Hello, Miss Saunders..." The PI's voice came through the tiny speaker. "I have some news for you."

Chapter Twenty

August 17

This is bad, Jade thought. She looked around the stunning venue, taking in the colorful domed ceiling and beautiful arches that made up this section of the Weylin. Rows of chairs parted in the middle to create an aisle that led to the raised platform. Jade would be marrying Spencer at that very spot in a few weeks. But, even with the knowledge, she didn't feel excited or even nervous. She was scared.

She fidgeted with the hemline of her neatly pressed charcoal dress. She and Spencer had taken a car to the Weylin as soon as the workday had ended, so she was still in her work clothes, sensible flats, and wore a tight ponytail. Spencer was also in his usual black suit with a crisp gray tie that was only a few shades lighter than her own clothes. Jade looked up to the ceiling again and felt a flutter in her stomach. God, she wished that it were butterflies.

"What's on your mind?" Spencer asked softly, coming up behind her and wrapping his arms around her waist. That made Jade smile, if only for a moment. She debated whether or not to answer his question with the truth. She didn't want to run the risk of upsetting him any more than he already was. But if she lied, he would know, and they were both tired of lies by this point.

"The one thing that shouldn't be," she said honestly. "Stacy." From the corner of her eyes she saw Kindall heading their way. Unlike them, Kindall was here on what was supposed to be her day off. She was dressed in dark designer jeans, tennis shoes and a maroon shirt with some quote scrawled in cursive that Jade couldn't be bothered to read. Spencer looked down at Jade like he wanted to say something but didn't have time.

"I managed to wade through the caterers offering to host the wedding," she said, not looking up from her tablet. "And the cake will be done in plenty of time. Linens are ordered, your dress is being altered as we speak, and—"

"Kindall," Jade interrupted, "thank you for everything. We both really appreciate it but we're not in any rush." Kindall finally looked up, the stress evident on her face.

"I work best under pressure," she said, "and this needs to be perfect."

"I think what Jade meant was don't overdo it," Spencer cut in. "Everything is already perfect and it doesn't all have to be done today. Hell, it doesn't all have to be done this week. And I trust that you've already taken care of everything at this point. We both hate to see you working when you've more than earned a day off."

"Thank you, but I promise you both that I'm here because I want to be. Even if I'd stayed home, I'd still be working on this wedding." Kindall smiled warmly and once again began tapping on the screen in front of her. Knowing that neither of them could change her mind about it, Spencer released Jade and began walking down the aisle, his eyes fixed on the ceiling just as Jade had done before. Kindall stopped working and came to stand beside Jade.

"So, what's the real problem here?" she asked. "Spill." Jade smiled, kind of glad to have someone other than Paige or Spencer to talk with about it. Kindall had been there for most of the drama, so it made sense that she would be so invested. *She needs to know these things for security reasons anyway, right?*

"I'm worried about Stacy," Jade said softly. The echo in the room was great for acoustics, not so much for secrets. "Ever since we got the results back, I've had this recurring nightmare of her showing up and burning this place to the ground."

"You're right to be worried," Kindall said. "Anyone willing to fake a pregnancy with someone like Spencer Alexander doesn't have limits. There's no telling what she's capable of." It wasn't what Jade had wanted to hear, but at least Kindall was telling the truth. "That being said, I don't think she'll do something quite that extreme."

"I wish we knew where she was. It would make me feel a million times better." When they had received the call from Dylan that had proved Stacy had faked the documents, Spencer's first action had been to call her. There had been no answer either then or since. Had she known that they were investigating? Was this some sort of elaborate scare tactic? Either way, Jade didn't trust that Stacy would disappear like that. She had to be planning something.

The ring of a cell phone echoed through the Weylin and Jade looked to Kindall to see if it was her phone. Kindall shrugged then pointed to Spencer. He had only allowed one ring before answering. He was too far away for them to hear what was being said, but Jade knew from his suddenly stiff posture that it wasn't good news. After a clipped goodbye, he hung up and turned to Jade and Kindall.

"That was Paige," he said as he walked over to them. "She's on her way over."

"Why did she call you instead of me?" Jade couldn't help asking. Only after the words had left her mouth did she realize how offended she'd sounded.

"Because she's with Stacy, and Stacy doesn't know you're here." Spencer smirked. "Apparently, Paige tracked her down and is bringing her right to us. She still doesn't know what we know, but Paige said she acted suspicious when it was brought up."

"Where has she been the last two weeks?" Kindall asked. She waited eagerly, despite Spencer's quizzical look and hesitance to continue.

"Kindall's a part of this, now." Jade crossed her arms and waited for him to answer.

"I don't know. But they're both on their way here to tell us." Spencer typed something into his phone before tucking it away in his pocket. "Shouldn't be long."

"Should I go?" Jade was already hoisting her purse higher on her shoulder. She didn't think it wise to be around Stacy right now, especially since she still didn't know what Spencer intended to do. At first, he'd just planned to tell her off and threaten her with a restraining order. But with her unexplained absence, there was no telling.

"Stay," he said. There was an intensity in his voice that Jade hadn't heard in long time. His gaze was focused on the front door. Jade and Kindall followed suit, the three of them waiting for whatever was about to come. Jade could hear a pin drop in the silence that followed. As the minutes ticked by, Jade was itching to fill the quiet with something, even if it was idle chatter. She shuffled her feet, shifting her weight nervously, but she found herself focused on the door as well.

As the handle turned and light began to seep into the entrance, Spencer grasped Jade's hand, squeezing it in a reassuring manner. Paige and Stacy walked in together, laughing about something. When Paige met Jade's eyes, though, her laughter stopped and was replaced with a nearly sinister look that made Jade almost feel bad for Stacy. Jade couldn't help but wonder what Paige had said to lure Stacy there.

"What are we doing here?" Stacy asked. She scanned the room before she saw Spencer. Her face fell ever-so-slightly before she forced a grin. "Spence!" Stacy cried, sprinting across the room to him. Her steps were wobbly, as though she didn't have full control of them. She slowed when she noticed Jade and Kindall on either side of him. Paige stealthily moved behind Stacy, blocking her only clear exit. Realization dawned and Jade watched Stacy's face rearrange again several times, first assuming an annoyed look, then confused, before finally landing on something meant to elicit pity. "Spence, my phone broke and I haven't been able to—"

"She broke it," Paige said in a flat tone, "when the wedding was confirmed to the media." Stacy spun around, no doubt to glare at Paige, and she stumbled a bit. Paige smiled sweetly. "You might as well tell them the truth before I do." Stacy obviously hadn't known what Paige and Jade were to each other. If she had, she never would have trusted her.

"No," Spencer said. "How about *I* tell the truth." He released his grip on Jade's hand and stepped toward Stacy, his hands clasped behind his back. "I don't care what you have to say. It's over, Stacy. This whole thing is over. We know that you forged the papers and that this was all some plan to split up Jade and me." Stacy looked to be on the verge of tears, but she never took her eyes from Spencer's.

"This ends one of two ways," he continued. "You can walk out of this building and never show your face to me or anyone I care about, or I can get the police involved and bring all your slanderous lies into the open. As it stands, everyone will know that you lied about being pregnant anyway, but I won't involve the authorities. Don't make it worse for yourself."

"T-this isn't my fault, Spencer," Stacy finally said tersely. Her cheeks were flushed red and she stammered over her words. "I wanted you to l-love me."

"You can't force someone to love you, Stacy. And if you actually cared about me, you wouldn't have gone about things the way you did." Spencer straightened his jacket and slid his hands into his pockets, his tone deepening even more. "I only wanted to let you know face to face that if you try anything else, I *will* ruin you…completely. And you know I have that power."

Stacy's lower lip trembled. She looked trapped, like she wanted to say or do something but was at a loss. Now that she had been standing close to her, Jade could smell the alcohol on the woman.

Spencer was maybe about a foot away. Stacy reared back and slapped him right across his face, snapping his head to the side. The sharp sound lingered in the air. No one dared move. Spencer swept back a strand of hair that had fallen from the force but made no move to otherwise defend himself.

"I'll forgive that because you're obviously drunk. You've hit the bottom, Stacy, and I'm done." His voice was the dangerous quiet that made the room feel a few degrees cooler. Stacy, in her defiance, looked like she might swing again, but Spencer walked away from her before she had the chance. Stacy huffed and approached Paige, waiting for her to move out of the way.

"Excuse me," Stacy said through gritted teeth. Paige looked to Jade for confirmation, and she nodded. Paige stood aside and Stacy left, sniffling and—for some reason—conjuring a limp.

"Do you think this is over?" Jade asked.

"I sure hope so," he replied.

"Holy crap, I had no idea what was about to happen!" Paige said as she ran up to Jade. "Do you think she'll come back? We should chase her down, do a little damage. Hi-*ya*!" Paige began to karate chop the air, kicking at the non-existent enemy.

"Calm down, Paige," Jade laughed. "It's finished and I don't intend to waste one more second on her. Is there anything else you need from us, Kindall? We've already booked this place, and seeing it in person hasn't changed our minds."

"I got a show I didn't buy a ticket for. I don't need anything else." The event coordinator waved them away, her attention taken by the tablet once again. Jade shrugged and turned to her friends. Spencer kept having to push the rebellious strand of hair from his forehead, and his cheek was now tinged pink.

"I have an idea," Paige said. "Let's get our minds off this. If you guys are done here, we can call Clint and see the sights? I know there are a few places I've been wanting to visit." Jade looked to Spencer, who stiffened at Clint's name. He hadn't been happy with Clint to begin with, but, after learning about his involvement with Stacy, he had been fuming. It had taken a lot of convincing to make Spencer see that Clint wasn't the bad guy. *How ironic.*

To his credit, Spencer forced a bored expression, shrugged and pulled his phone out again to call a car. Suddenly, Kindall was standing by their side, her tablet put away and keys in hand.

"I heard something about a tour and Clint," she said. "I can drive."

Chapter Twenty-One

August 25

Jade extended her arms above her head, turning her neck until she heard the satisfying *pop* then relaxing back into her chair. It was always nice to have a fully completed workday, and she was looking forward to a hot shower and soft bed as soon as possible. She had stayed later than usual, with the sun already past the towers in the distance, but her to-do list for the day had everything marked off, so that was a win.

She looked out over the dark-blue sky that was tinged with orange, appreciating the view for a few glorious seconds before she began collecting her things. There was a knock on her office door. Through the glass, Jade saw Spencer holding his phone up. She smiled as he let himself in.

"Got your text," he said. "I just finished up, too." He stood just inside the door, waiting for her to gather her belongings. When she made to leave, he remained in her way. "I have a surprise for you."

"Is it a massage? Because I would love that." Jade smiled tiredly at him, but he just took her hand, leading her away from the offices and up to their penthouse. Once inside, he instructed her to go upstairs.

"Get ready, Jade," he said, "for a night you won't forget." As exhausted as she was, Jade couldn't say no. There was only a week to go before the wedding, but it seemed like the closer it got, the less and less she saw of Spencer, so she was grateful for any time they got to spend together — even if it meant missing out on much-needed rest. When she reached their bedroom, she found a dress already laid out for her. It was a floor-length white dress with intricate beading along the body, fading down into the hem. The dress was sleeveless and backless, with a modest halter neckline. Beside it sat complementing jewelry and a pair of Jade's own white pumps.

Jade showered and dressed quickly. She didn't know what Spencer had planned, but she couldn't wait to find out. She briefly entertained the notion that Spencer might have planned an elopement. Then, she recalled how much work had gone into the wedding and dismissed the thought. After blow-drying and twisting her hair up into an elegant bun, she put on the earrings and a bracelet, then did her makeup. With one last nervous look into the mirror, she went to find Spencer.

The sky was dark and spotted with stars when Jade came downstairs. Spencer was waiting for her, hands in the pockets of his tailored suit. His hair was still damp from a shower and he wore a stark red tie. *He must have used the guest room to get himself ready*, she thought. Spencer took her in, trailing his blue eyes over every inch of her. When his gaze met hers, he grinned.

"I would say you look beautiful, but that would be an understatement."

Jade blushed, a small laugh escaping her lips.

"In fact, I don't think there's a single word in the English language to describe how wonderful you are."

"So, what happens now?" she asked. Spencer didn't answer, only offered his hand for her, taking her back toward the elevator and to the ground floor. Jade didn't say anything, content to let him have his fun. She also noticed a new energy that came with the anticipation and erased the fatigue from the long day. Spencer took her outside of the building, where a black and silver Audi R8 was parked by the curb.

"I figured it would be more interesting if we got to where we're going in style," Spencer said, upon seeing Jade's stunned expression. He opened the passenger side door for her, helping her in like a gentleman and gently closing the door behind her. Jade adjusted herself on the comfortable black leather seats. Spencer climbed in beside her and Jade realized that she had never seen him drive before. She had assumed he could, of course, but had never witnessed it for herself.

Spencer pressed a large red button on the steering wheel and the engine roared to life. Jade had never seen Spencer like this. He was like a kid in a candy store, nearly bouncing in his seat at the opportunity to drive. He pulled out onto the street, which was still a little jammed with traffic. Spencer didn't seem to mind, though, content to follow the other cars slowly.

"Will you tell me where we're going?" Jade asked.

"We're going to your favorite place for dinner," Spencer said casually. "Sushi Ginza Onodera." Jade groaned and let her head fall back on the seat. It had been her and Spencer's first outing together — and it was her least-favorite food. Still, she would play along. Maybe, if she were in New York long enough, she would even develop a taste for raw fish.

Jade turned to stare out of the window as they passed by what used to be Stacy's store. It was dark and empty with a red *'For Sale'* sign displayed in the window. It hadn't taken long for certain prominent people to hear about what she'd done, especially not with Paige and Kindall spreading the word without any prompting from Jade or Spencer. Within two days of their final meeting, Stacy had packed up and moved back home, wherever that was. Jade breathed a deep sigh of relief. Things could have been much worse.

The congestion on the street began to disperse and Spencer was able to drive at what she could imagine was his ideal speed. The purring engine could have lulled Jade to sleep if she weren't so curious about whatever Spencer had planned. It took no time for them to arrive at the restaurant, where Spencer parked the car then escorted Jade into the building.

Even though it had been nearly two months since their last visit, the place still held a familiar air to it. There were differences that Jade spotted, though. The lights were dimmed even more, and they were the only customers this time around. The two chefs stood behind the bar, smiling at them. Soft, relaxing music was playing faintly in the background.

Spencer immediately greeted the chefs in their native tongue before he pulled out Jade's chair for her. Two glasses were set out in front of them, followed by Spencer's usual dish of sashimi and a bowl of traditional ramen for Jade.

"They didn't have this last time we were here," she whispered to Spencer. She thanked the two men, who then disappeared to the back room.

"I might have paid them to make an exception," he said, picking up his chopsticks. She looked back at Spencer. His actions so far could be read as innocent, but Jade knew there was more to it. She crossed her arms, raising one hand to tap a finger on her bottom lip in thought.

"All right, spill it," Jade said. "What is all of this?" Spencer looked up and shrugged, as if he had no idea what she was talking about. "Come on. We never do this. You're up to something and I want to know what it is. Are we eloping tonight? Is that it?"

Spencer chuckled, taking a long drink of his water.

"You'll know when it's time," he said. "Trust me, okay?" Jade was still skeptical, but gave in. If nothing else, she was glad to have this time with Spencer away from work. Here, they were a couple out for a date, and that was refreshing in and of itself. Jade snapped her chopsticks together and began to carefully scoop up the savory noodles. They were steaming, filling and cooked to perfection. If she could order this every time they came here, she wouldn't mind visiting more often.

She thought sadly about how the two of them had been working overtime since the day after negotiations, meeting up at night for takeout and usually falling asleep on the couch. Then they were up early the next morning to do it all over again. It was a cycle Jade had been used to and thrived on, but now it made her feel distant from Spencer, which was something she was still struggling to understand.

As Jade and Spencer ate, someone would occasionally come refill their drinks, but other than that, they were left alone. No other customers came in during that time, and Jade realized that he had bought the restaurant out for the night. Each time one of the men would come out, Spencer watched him with a skeptical eye. It finally reached a point where Jade had to mention it.

"He's not doing anything wrong, is he?" she asked. Spencer looked at her and answered with a serious expression.

"I don't like the way he's looking at you." Jade stared him then let out a small laugh. When Spencer didn't join her, she only laughed harder.

"You're not joking? Spence, you're cute when you get all possessive, but don't take it out on them. They're being polite and doing their jobs." Spencer didn't look convinced. "I promise you that even if they were up to no good, I wouldn't trade you for the world."

That seemed to do the trick and, once Spencer had been placated, dinner was exquisite. They began to talk, reminiscing about their childhood adventures. About halfway through dinner, a bottle of ice-cold sake was brought out to them. Jade began to wish it would last forever. She loved seeing Spencer laugh, the kind of laugh that made his eyes practically glow and made her laugh in return. After two glasses, the sake bubbled in her stomach, causing her to feel giddy. Jade had watched Spencer and noted that he only drank one.

There was a moment, as they were finishing up, that she caught Spencer watching her. He had his elbow on the table, his chin propped up on his hand. His oceanic gaze was fixed on her, observing her like the main attraction in a gallery showing that he just had to have. She was about to make a quip about how a picture would last longer, when Spencer spoke up.

"When we're done here, there's one more thing I want to show you."

Jade was curious as to what other surprises he'd planned for the night. She placed her chopsticks across her empty bowl and pushed it away. Spencer stood and offered her his arm, calling out what she assumed was a 'thank you' to the men in the back. The restaurant sat across the street from Bryant Park and that was exactly where Spencer led her. The night air was crisp and cool, the sounds of the city serving as a soothing white noise behind them. Jade and Spencer walked along a paved trail surrounded by green grass and orange trees. Alexander Tower was bright and extremely visible from the path they were on. The last time they'd been here, it had been the middle of the day. Now, late into the night, the park was lit with streetlamps and fairy lights strung along the tree trunks. There wasn't another person in sight as they strolled in silence.

"Let's sit," Spencer said, pointing to a bench ahead. "I'm sure your feet hurt in those shoes." It was true that they were bothering her a little, but Jade was more focused on how nervous Spencer was acting all of a sudden. The lamps caught light through the drops of water on the surrounding grass, making the ground itself seem to shimmer. She sat down carefully on the bench, while Spencer remained standing, his hands clasped behind his back.

"Is everything all right?" Jade asked. Spencer huffed a laugh and brushed his fingers through his hair.

"I started out so confident, but now..." He sat on the bench with Jade and looked out at the trees. "Now I don't know what to do." He reached into his pocket and pulled out a small black box. It was the same box that he'd tried to give Jade at the engagement party. "I was going to do this in the restaurant, but it didn't feel right. I wanted to be smooth about this, but I feel like I'm in high school again, trying to ask the most popular girl to the prom."

"Spence…" Jade didn't know what to say. She was moved by the gesture, even finding his jitters adorable. Now that she knew what this was, she was having a hard time containing her joy. Jade placed a reassuring hand on his shoulder. "You don't have to do anything fancy, Spence. Just tell me what you want to say." He looked at her, relief washing over his features.

"All right." Spencer knelt down on the sidewalk in front of her and opened the box. Inside sat a shining platinum band with a princess cut diamond. Two smaller diamonds were fixed on either side, and a swirling design was etched into the metal. It was simple yet beautiful and somehow still more than Jade had been expecting. Her breath caught as she met Spencer's eyes.

"Jade Saunders, I know that the only reason you came here was because of a contract," Spencer started. "Then you showed up and everything from before came flooding back and, against all odds, you gave me another chance. I know the contracts have been signed and you've technically been engaged to me for a while." He paused to take her hand in his. "But I wanted to do this right, with a ring I've chosen and with words from my heart.

"I love you more than you'll ever know, Jade. I have since we were kids right up until you told me you loved me. Even when we were apart all those years, there wasn't a day that passed by when I didn't think of you. I want to spend the rest of my days proving that. Jade, I want to spend the rest of my life with you. Will you allow me that honor?" Tears began to drip down her cheeks as she nodded. The wedding had been planned and would take place in a matter of days, but for Spencer to do this made her feel...loved. There was no more hesitation. There were no more doubts. She still loved Spencer and would never stop.

Spencer slid the ring onto her finger, and she threw her arms around his neck, dropping to her knees to cling to him. Her dream of running the company would be fulfilled in the coming months. Now, it had been replaced by a new dream.

As Jade held Spencer close, she thought about their future together, working side by side every day, having children and experiencing all the other joys in life that were laid out before them. Right now, the company didn't matter. The buyout didn't matter. All that was important was that they were, in this moment, together.

Epilogue

September 1

The ocean glimmered with the noon sun. Jade closed her eyes and let the cool breeze undo the hour of work that had gone into her hair. She was still wearing her gorgeous champagne wedding dress, the flare at the bottom lifting around her now-bare feet. Glancing to her left, Jade saw New York fading farther and farther away. She'd miss it more than she ever thought she would but was be happy to be away for a while. How she would sleep without the white noise, though, was a mystery.

Spencer smiled at her from the helm window and she quickly corrected that thought. She knew *exactly* how she would sleep. Jade left the sky lounge and stepped into the cool enclosed bridge to stand beside her now-husband, who was busy talking to the captain.

In order to let them fully enjoy their honeymoon, Carlton had loaned them *The Absolution* and hired staff to accommodate them on their mystery trip. After confirming their course with the captain — an attractive middle-aged man with a heavy Italian accent — Spencer turned to Jade.

"What's on your mind, Mrs. Alexander?" he asked. Jade shook her head but grinned at the new name. Spencer understood the silence and didn't press. Spencer and Kindall had planned the whole honeymoon as a surprise for Jade. Even though she wasn't fond of surprises, she appreciated the effort.

The wedding had gone off without a hitch, thanks to Kindall. Despite Jade's fears of Stacy showing up for one last attempt to win or to attack Spencer, the day had been calm and quite beautiful. Francine, Candace and Paige had shown up extra early to get ready with Jade, spending a couple of hours on hair, makeup and nails alone. By the time they were through, Jade hardly recognized herself. Her dress had been altered to fit her perfectly and flattered her natural curves. Her makeup was neutral, with a pop of amber around the eyes. She had looked and felt gorgeous.

She'd been driven to the Weylin but had been ushered inside without getting to see the main room. It had only been her and Paige there until her father had arrived to join her. Timothy's eyes had been red and glassy, like he'd already gotten a head start on crying.

'None of that,' Jade had said, struggling against her own tears as she straightened her veil. She'd dabbed at his eyes with a tissue from a side table, then wrapped him in a hug that he'd returned with full force. He'd told her how proud he was and how much he loved her. Then, it had been time for them to walk down the aisle together.

The soft tones of a violin had announced her arrival. Jade and Timothy walked past the double doors and everyone stood. Nervous jitters that had twisted Jade's stomach all morning had begun to loosen their grip as she took in the room around her.

Kindall had transformed the place into a magical autumn forest. Orange and yellow leaves hung elegantly from the ceiling. Fall flowers in warm colors had sprung out of benches and pillars placed around the room. An archway placed at the very front had been little more than a canopy of wildflowers edged with gold leaf.

All Jade's worries and fears had totally vanished when she'd seen Spencer. He'd been dressed in a classic black tuxedo with burgundy vest and accents, and his dark hair had been combed back. His eyes had sparkled when he'd seen her and a crooked, unfiltered grin had overtaken his face. Jade had blushed, suddenly self-conscious in her finery. A small part of her, the part that was still a teenager swooning over Spencer Alexander, had been screaming with sheer joy and disbelief that this was happening.

The reception had been a blur of photographs, cake and dancing. When they'd left, Paige had been the last one to see them off and Clint and Kindall had been suspiciously missing. Now, standing with her arms around Spencer's waist, looking over the ocean that was mirrored in his eyes, Jade felt that very same swell of emotion.

"Everything should be smooth sailing from here," he said with a wink. Jade rolled her eyes but laughed anyway. Even the captain, who had probably heard that joke more than he could imagine, gave a weak laugh.

They left the helm and were entering their room when Spencer's phone pinged that a message had arrived. He shut the door and pulled the device from his pocket to check.

"Everything all right?" Jade asked as his forehead furrowed in confusion.

"Fine," he answered as he scanned the screen. "Just the best man wishing us luck and...letting me know that he got his official acceptance letter into college!" Spencer's eyes widened as he began typing a reply to his brother.

"That's amazing!" An overwhelming rush of pride washed over her. Bryce was her brother, now, too. She peered over at the screen and caught that Bryce had thrown in that he was 'catching up to Spencer'. He finished typing back what was no doubt an equally taunting reply, then turned the phone off and tossed it into a chair.

"Now that that's done and we are on a straight shot to Ireland — " Jade lit up at the mention of a destination and, seeing her excitement, Spencer grinned down at her, his dimples flashing in that way she loved. He slid his fingers beneath the strap of her dress, tugging her toward him ever-so-gently. "You'll have to be patient. For now, there are more important matters to attend to."

"Well, Mr. Alexander," Jade said, sliding her hands over the smooth satin of his vest, "I, for one, can't wait."

Want to see more from this author?
Here's a taster for you to enjoy!

The Devil's Maverick
Lori Fayre

Excerpt

"Can you hear me? What's your name?" The voice was floating through the haze in Alva's mind, along with some buzzing and ringing in her ears. "Stay with me, all right?" it asked.

"Where am I?" she slurred. Her throat felt raw, like she'd swallowed sand. She opened her eyes, but the scant light was harsh. She looked down at her blurry, blood-soaked hands. She was sure she'd cleaned them. With a blink, her skin was back to its normal porcelain tone. Alva shut her eyes again. *What is going on?*

"You're safe for now," the voice said in answer to her question. "Here. Drink some water." Whoever it was put a glass bottle to her lips and she welcomed the cool liquid. She recalled choking on briny sea water and almost spat out the fresh. "There now… Rest. I'll be back to check on you later." She heard the person leave and tried to pull herself together.

She was on a ship. She could tell that much by the gentle rocking motion. But it wasn't the ship she had left the United States on. The boards were too creaky and it was far too dark. Not that she had been on some luxury boat to begin with, but this seemed a step down.

She could tell that she was sitting on a bare wooden floor with a blanket thrown over her lap. The last thing she remembered was... *Cannon fire. Screaming. Flames. Pirates!*

Alva opened her eyes suddenly and her head pounded. She looked frantically around what she now saw was a cell. Iron bars caged her and a solitary lantern lit the other empty keeps. The Royal Navy ship she had been stowed away on had been overrun by pirates, and she was now their prisoner. Her breathing picked up. I'm being held captive.

Alva pulled the tattered blanket over her in a façade of protection. Her clothes were damp and freezing from where she had fallen into the ocean. They must have fished her out. But why would they do that when it must have been one of their own who had thrown her overboard in the first place? She couldn't recall his face, but the more she thought about it, the less she really wanted to know his reasoning. She'd seen plenty of people who'd been kidnapped and forced into slavery. By the time they had been released or escaped, there hadn't been much left of them.

She closed her eyes again and rested her head against the wall of the brig. She'd just wanted to start over, to have a new life. Now, odds were she was going to die. There was nothing she could do about it at the moment, though. She was weak and exhausted, her entire body aching. She would have to wait for the inevitable. Maybe she could get away before something too awful happened to her. Eventually, the fatigue took over and she drifted off to sleep.

Alva's dreams were drenched in blood, fire and screams. Memories of the attack resurfaced and mingled with older memories that she'd tried to lock away. The blood on her hands became tacky then crusty. Somewhere, a bell rang. Someone needed her upstairs. No, it wasn't a bell…

The jingling of keys woke Alva. She checked her hands, but they were clean. She could see a small form on the other side of the iron bars and heard the click of a lock. She started to get up but froze when she heard someone else coming down a flight of steps. The smaller person swung the gate to her cell open with a high creak.

"Feeling better?" the voice from earlier asked. It was deep and clear, with a crisp accent straight from the high-end of London. The lantern was still lit in the corner and Alva could now see the smaller man clearly. He was elderly, stooped under the weight of a hunched back and had a kind face. He smiled sadly at her and she noticed some of his teeth were missing. Then, he limped around the room, lighting the rest of the lanterns along the walls.

From the flames, Alva could see that the other cells weren't empty but were used for storage. None of the soldiers from the ship had been taken. If they had, they certainly weren't being kept here. From what she could tell, these weren't the type of pirates to take quarter. Soon, the second man before Alva came into focus. It was a slow process, but she finally got her first good look at him.

He was tall, dressed in black trousers, boots and a blood-red silk shirt. He had a long, black leather coat and wore matching gloves. With more light, she saw a mess of dark curly hair rippling past his shoulders and framing his elegant features. His silver eyes pierced through her and a cocky smile played on his lips.

"Welcome aboard *The Diablo*, Miss," he said. "My name is Elijah Maverick and I am the captain."

Alva snapped her mouth shut from where her jaw had dropped. She hadn't counted on this at all. Elijah Maverick—the pirate her town and the entire coast feared—had kidnapped her and was holding her against her will. Her stomach turned when the imposing man stared at her, as though waiting for something.

"Your name, please," he said, seeming rather amused. "Give me your name."

"Alva," she finally said. It would make things easier if she just went along with him. This wasn't her usual take on things, as her former employer could have told them. She was the one who usually challenged anyone with whom she disagreed, but, under the circumstances, playing the game this way might very well save her life. "Alva Grace Eastman."

"Well, Miss Eastman"—he took a step closer—"I'm here to welcome you onto my ship, as you will be staying with us for quite some time."

"How long will that be?" she couldn't help but ask.

His eyes glinted mischievously. "Until I decide otherwise," he answered.

"Why?"

"Something about you intrigues me, my dear." She wanted to ask what he meant by that, but he silenced her by holding up a hand. "And, contrary to what you may have heard, I'm not in the habit of killing innocents. Any questions you have may be asked later. For now, I've brought you some dry clothes to put on. You'll die of hypothermia if you stay in those." He tossed a bundle of fabric at her. "I'll leave you to get dressed." He beckoned the elderly man to join him and they went up the stairs, leaving her alone again.

"At least it's not dark anymore," Alva said aloud to herself. She shed her old dress as quickly as possible and threw on what he had left for her. She was sure her new clothes were a lot more expensive than those she was used to, but they fit as though they had been tailored just for her. She laced up the front of the blue dress and pushed her long, wavy dark-brown hair back from her face. Then she pulled on her boots, which were still a little damp, and took a few moments to examine her surroundings.

The foolish notion of hiding behind some of the barrels stacked against the far wall passed through her mind and she nearly laughed aloud at her stupidity. Judging by the faint voices just outside the door at the stairs, Elijah and his man were staying close. Besides, hiding would get her nowhere but dead.

"I'm dressed," she called out through the open door. She wasn't sure what to do, but she imagined that just walking out and meeting them at the steps might go over as well as hiding would. Elijah and his friend came back down to her level and the captain looked at her with a curious expression.

"You truly are beautiful, Miss Eastman," he said. Alva tilted her head in confusion and wondered what could possibly make him say that. He seemed to realize what he'd said and was quick to add, "When you don't look like a drowned rat, at any rate. You may come out now." She took a small step toward him. "I won't hurt you," he assured her, but his smile suggested otherwise.

Elijah took her arm and made a gesture with his free hand for her to precede him up the steps. The old man shuffled behind them, grasping the railing tightly with his gnarled fingers. She wondered how on earth someone like him had ended up there. She stopped just before reaching the sunlight and turned to the captain.

He sighed and looked at her as if he'd been expecting this.

"Will I be able to ask my questions soon?" she asked.

"You may ask one now. Only one."

Alva sorted through the list she had been compiling in her head and chose the most pressing issue, her future on board the vessel.

"What do you intend to do with me?"

He flashed a wolfish grin that was more than a little intimidating. The silence that followed seemed to stretch on for hours.

"What do you think, Miss Eastman?" he asked smoothly.

"I have no idea," she answered somewhat honestly. "But I know what you are. You're a pirate. There's no telling what you have planned."

He shrugged in mock innocence.

"Nothing I think you can't handle. Follow me," he said, urging her up the last few steps without any real explanation. Her knees felt weak from fear. She resolved that she would try to hide how terrified she really was. If she let her guard down, the horrible scenarios her imagination was coming up with might come to life. And he had a bit of a surprise coming, because she was stronger than he probably expected.

Home of Erotic Romance

Sign up for our newsletter and find out about all our romance book releases, eBook sales and promotions, sneak peeks and FREE romance books!

About the Author

Lori Fayre was born and raised in a small South Georgia town. Her debut novel, "The Devil's Maverick", was a novel nearly six years in the making. An obsessive consumer of historical romance, Lori knew it was the genre she wanted to write. When she's not writing, she enjoys reading, drawing, or binging Hulu with her husband and Yorkie.

Lori loves to hear from readers. You can find her contact information, website details and author profile page at https://www.totallybound.com